KATIE'S CAKES

KATIE'S CAKES

•

Helen Spears

AVALON BOOKS
NEW YORK

PRINTED IN THE UNITED STATES OF AMERICA
ON ACID-FREE PAPER
BY HADDON CRAFTSMEN, BLOOMSBURG, PENNSYLVANIA

To Mary, J.O. and Leslie, and to David, whose light still shines from afar.

The palm trees wave beneath the breeze,
And falsely promise lifelong ease.
But hearts are broken over there,
And finding love is all too rare.

Chapter One

Anywhere else in the world, this weather would be too good to be true. The sun shone in a cloudless blue sky, shimmering on the tips of the magenta bougainvillea right outside her door. The temperature hovered around seventy-five degrees, and would get no warmer than eighty or eighty-two at the most. Only four blocks away the white-capped surf of the ocean rocked gently against the warm sand. On such a day in May, anywhere else in the world, people would be overcome with an uncontrollable case of spring fever. In Honolulu, however, it was just another perfect day.

To Katie Weston, it was one of the worst days of her life. She stood at the door of her office, adjacent to her kitchen. Her hair was caught up in a hairnet, and there was flour and a smudge of chocolate on her cheek. She wore no makeup and there were dark circles under her eyes from lack of sleep. She had been up since 3:00 A.M., trying to get an order ready on time.

Now there was an officer at the door demanding to see the proprietor. She had already explained that she couldn't possibly take an order for a cake to be delivered the following Saturday—she was booked three weeks in advance, and was desperately trying to keep on schedule.

As they talked, the timer on the oven buzzed. "Excuse me. I have to take care of this." She hurried to the kitchen, snapped off the oven, and took out three layers of wedding cake. She inhaled the sweet fragrance of the cakes, and put them on the rack to cool.

"What time does this Katie come in?"

That's when she realized he had followed her into the kitchen. She turned and led the way back out to the office.

"*I'm* Katie, and I told you I can't possibly take another order for next Saturday. My assistant just quit, and I'm in a real jam trying to do all this myself. Sorry."

He gave her a sympathetic look. "Well, I can see you have a problem."

She liked the warmth of his voice. He sounded genuinely concerned. And she supposed all men looked handsome in uniform. This one certainly did . . . tall and lean, with perfect military posture.

"You know, I have a problem, too. Admiral Bronfman doesn't accept second best. I've been put in charge of getting a cake for his retirement party, and if I show up with an ordinary bakery cake I'll be killed."

She smiled at his earnest expression. "You're exaggerating."

"Well, I'll at least be put in irons and maybe even court-martialed."

"Oh, come now."

"Everyone says you're the best." His eyes were pleading.

"Did anyone ever tell you you're the most persistent person who ever lived?"

"Sorry, but I'm fighting for my life here."

"Will you stop that? I'm fighting for my life, too. This is the third person who has quit on me, and for no reason at all. I'm very considerate, I'm pleasant to be around, and I pay more than McDonalds. Why do they always quit?"

"Where do you find all these unreliable assistants?"

"Through ads in the local paper, word of mouth, anywhere I can. There are plenty of young girls who need work."

He was thoughtful for a moment, then his expression brightened. "Would you take my order if I found you another assistant?"

"That's an offer I couldn't refuse, but I need help in a hurry. I've been up since three o'clock this morning, and I'm about to drop. Each order is for a special occasion, and it's essential that they be delivered on time. If I don't get this cake ready in time for Colonel Howell's daughter's wedding this afternoon..." Her voice broke. "Well, you get the picture."

"May I use your phone?"

"Sure." She motioned towards the phone on the counter. "I need to start the frosting. I'll be in the kitchen."

She was proud of her kitchen. It boasted the latest in professional equipment, gleaming white and stainless steel, and it had cost a fortune.

The rest of the house was the usual flimsy island construction, located in a rather poor neighborhood. She knew she wouldn't have been able to afford it before the Japanese economic upheaval, which knocked the bottom out of the local economy.

The kitchen and her new van, which were necessary for deliveries, constituted the biggest part of the bank loan that made her business possible. If it failed she stood to lose everything she had, and more.

She whipped up the white chocolate buttercream frosting. This would be one of her most exquisite cakes, with an icing wreath of flowers and leaves spiraling around the entire cake.

As she became engrossed in the design, she completely forgot about the officer waiting in her office. She was startled when she heard a voice behind her. "Hey, that's beautiful."

"Oh, I didn't hear you come in. It's a wedding cake."

"It's great, but not for Admiral Bronfman."

"I told you . . ."

He didn't let her finish. "Would twelve o'clock be soon enough for your new assistant to start?"

She stared at him. "Are you kidding?"

"Of course not. Nina Ellison works at the Officer's Club three nights a week. Her husband left her with a load of bills, and she needs more work."

Katie heaved a big sigh of relief, and smiled. "Well, in that case, let's do business." She motioned toward a table by the door. "There's a catalog of cakes I have made. Go through that and see what appeals to you. I'll be with you just as soon as I can find a stopping place here."

He took the catalog and returned to the office, where he sat down and leafed through it. He had just gone through all twenty-seven pages when she came around the counter and took out her order form.

"Sorry to keep you waiting. Are you ready to order?"

"Well, yes and no. You see, Admiral Bronfman is a very picky person. He has his own particular likes and dislikes, and I wouldn't want to get something that wouldn't please him."

"Of course not. There's a very nice devil's food cake in there that men seem to like a lot."

"Oh, he doesn't like chocolate."

"Well then, how about butterscotch?"

"That's a possibility. Can you dress it up with something special?"

"A naval insignia would be appropriate. . . . an anchor, for instance. Does anything else come to mind?"

"Oh yes, he loves macadamia nuts."

"Great. How about a butterscotch-macadamia nut cake?"

"That sounds good." He showed her a chocolate cake in the catalog. "If you could make it kind of like that, only with butterscotch, I think that would be perfect."

She took her pen and order form. "Your name?"

"Lieutenant commander Camden Carter."

A smile crossed her lips and she turned her head, but not before he noticed.

"I wasn't a lieutenant commander when my mother named me, but that's one reason I'm working hard to be an admiral some day."

"Sorry, it's really a very nice name. This will be ready by two o'clock next Saturday afternoon. Shall I deliver it to the Officer's Club?"

"Yes. Should I pay you then?"

She nodded and gave him his receipt, and she thanked him for his business. "I'm sorry you caught me in the midst of a crisis. Thanks for your help."

"That's okay. I hope everything works out well with Nina. I think you'll like her."

She watched as he left, admiring his military bearing, and his wide shoulders, and smiled as he turned and gave her a jaunty salute. Something about his grin told her he had known all along he would talk her into taking his order.

Chapter Two

It was high noon when a tall, sandy-haired woman in her early forties appeared in Katie's office.

Katie wiped her hands on a towel, a hopeful expression on her face. "Hello. You must be Nina Ellison."

The woman stared at her uncertainly. "Are you Katie?"

"Yes. Lieutenant commander Carter said you were looking for a job."

"That's right. I am a quick learner if you'll give me a chance."

"Great. I'm a little shorthanded right now, and I'm having a hard time keeping up with my orders. As soon as I finish dec-

9

orating the wedding cake I'm working on, I need to deliver it this afternoon. When can you start?"

"How about right now?"

"Wonderful. I'm afraid I can only pay a little more than minimum wage. Is that a problem?"

"I can manage with that. I work at the Officer's Club three nights a week, so I can't stay late those nights."

"Yes, lieutenant commander Carter told me you worked there. Come on into the kitchen and I'll show you around."

Nina glanced at the kitchen and gave a low whistle under her breath. "You have quite a nice layout here."

"Thank you. I'm sure you realize the importance of cleanliness in this business. You'll need to wear a hairnet in the kitchen, mop the floor and clean the counters."

"Of course. You know, you have quite a reputation. It's no wonder you're so busy."

"That's what I told lieutenant commander Carter. I must say, he is just about the most persistent person I've ever met."

Nina looked her straight in the eye, and spoke with finality. "Lieutenant commander Carter is one of the finest gentlemen I've ever met."

Katie smiled. The message was clear: she would brook no criticism of Camden Carter. There seemed to be some kind of bond there.

"You'll find a clean smock and some hairnets in that drawer there. I'm almost finished with this cake, then I'll deliver it."

Nina hesitated a moment as she looked her over. "Uh . . . I expect you'll want to fix up a bit before you make your delivery, won't you?"

Katie looked down at her stained smock and, for the first time, became aware of how she must look. "I guess I must be a mess."

"Don't worry," Nina said tactfully, "I'll clean up in here while you make yourself presentable."

Katie finished her decorating, then placed the cake in its plastic carrying case. "There, that's all finished. I'll be back in a few minutes."

* * *

One look in the full-length mirror on her bathroom door made her do a double-take. Her beautiful dark hair, usually so shiny, was hidden under a hairnet. Her face, completely devoid of makeup, was streaked with flour and chocolate, and the dark circles under her eyes emphasized her fatigue. She hadn't seen anything so scary since Halloween.

As she stood under the warm shower, she gave a wry little laugh. While she was busy admiring the handsome lieutenant commander Carter, he was probably thinking she was the most revolting thing he had ever seen. Oh well, she didn't have time for romance anyway, no matter how tempted she might be.

Already feeling better, she dressed quickly in a pair of crisp white slacks and a navy blue shirt. Who knows, she just might survive this crisis yet.

Katie placed the cake securely in the van and set out for the Officer's Club. By this time the temperature hovered at eighty. She switched on the air conditioning and the radio. Soothing island music filled the air, and she felt the tension slip away.

She liked what she saw of Nina. She seemed to be a decent woman, hard-working and loyal, who had not been treated well by fate. What was her connection with Camden? As she drove slowly along the road which ran between the hotels and the beach, she took care to avoid a throng of tourists.

Once she reached the Officer's Club, she parked at the rear, and removed the cake from the back. The air was warm and heavy, laden with the smell of seaweed and kelp from the nearby beach. Clouds scudded overhead, and she knew that any moment an unexpected tropical shower would come, to be gone as quickly as it came.

She hurriedly entered the delivery door, told the attendant she was from Katie's Cakes, and that the delivery was for the Howell wedding this afternoon.

"Yes, we've been expecting you." He turned and found an envelope marked Katie's Cakes, and handed it to her. "Mrs. Howell was nervous, but I told her you were always right on time."

"Thank you."

As she drove back home, she smiled. He might not have been so sure of that if he had seen her kitchen last night.

With Nina's help, Katie spent the rest of the week getting organized, and she finally felt like her business was running efficiently. If Nina proved to be as reliable as she appeared, Katie felt she could increase her output. She could even give Nina a raise once she felt absolutely certain she wouldn't be deserted.

They had talked about why so many of her assistants had quit. As Katie explained, "If I had any inkling of why they left, I would certainly do something about it."

Nina shook her head, puzzled. "I can't figure it out. It isn't anything you've done. If you treated them as well as you've treated me, then they should have been glad to work for you."

Katie took extra care with Admiral Bronfman's cake. She was determined to make it the most wonderful cake she had ever made. Of course, she always did her best, but for this one she went all out. She was anxious to erase the terrible first impression she had made on Camden Carter.

After lunch, Nina didn't have to remind her to fix up before she made her delivery. She showered and dressed in her usual crisp white slacks and navy shirt, but this time she carefully styled her thick dark hair, which fell in soft curls to her shoulders. Her makeup was subtle, emphasizing her dark eyes and her creamy complexion.

The effect, as she glanced in her full-length mirror, was entirely uncalculated. As an afterthought, she dabbed just a tiny bit of perfume on her pulse points. *Take that, Camden Carter!* she thought, breathing in the sensuous fragrance.

When she walked into the kitchen, Nina looked up and whistled. "My, don't you clean up nicely!"

"Thanks. I'm going to deliver Admiral Bronfman's cake. If he doesn't like it, then he really is a grouch."

"Oh, he'll like it all right."

The Officer's Club was out some way, and as she drove, Katie couldn't keep her mind off Lieutenant commander Carter. Was he really as attractive as she remembered? Or had she been too woozy with fatigue to see clearly? She couldn't stop thinking of her first meeting with Camden.

Finally she pulled into the delivery entrance, and brought the cake into the club. A young officer took the cake. "Nice," he murmured, then handed her an envelope. "Lieutenant commander Carter said to give you this."

"Thank you. I had hoped to have a word with him."

"He's in the next room setting up for the party. Hold on and I'll get him." The young officer turned and went to the adjacent room, where the sound of voices escaped when the door was opened.

Camden came toward her expectantly, and as he came nearer, his expression changed. He stared, looking puzzled, then smiled. His voice sounded uncertain. "Katie?"

"I just dropped off Admiral Bronfman's cake. I hope he likes it."

Camden glanced at the cake. "He will—it's beautiful."

"I wanted to speak to you so I could thank you for sending me Nina. She's wonderful, just what I needed. I can't thank you enough."

"I knew you'd like her. She's a gem." He continued to stare at her. "You look so . . . different," he finished lamely.

Katie smiled. "I guess I didn't make much of a first impression. Well, I just wanted to thank you. I'd better get back." She turned to go.

Before she reached the door, Camden had caught up with her. "Wait. I . . . well, it's awfully late, I know, but it just so happens I don't have a date for Admiral Bronfman's retirement party tonight. I guess you're probably busy, though?"

"Are you asking me to be your guest at the party tonight?"

"Yes. Please."

She smiled. "I'd be delighted to be your date tonight. Thanks to Nina, everything is under control at work, and I'm feeling almost human."

"Great. I'll pick you up at seven-fifteen."

Driving home, it occurred to Katie that a man as attractive as Camden must have his choice of dates, so why wouldn't he have a date for such an important occa-

sion as his commanding officer's retirement?

On the other hand, she thought, *count
your blessings, and don't question fate.*

Chapter Three

Katie did her best to keep calm as she dressed for the admiral's retirement party. She wore a long dress of deep azure blue with a side slit. The effect was quite sophisticated, and the color emphasized her peaches and cream complexion. Altogether very effective, she had to admit.

As she worked on her hair, she thought of Camden's impromptu invitation. There must have been dozens of women in his circle of friends who would have been thrilled to go with him, yet he hadn't invited any of them. Perhaps he thought he would be too busy with the details of the party to entertain a date.

If that was his thinking, she reasoned, then why did he change his mind and ask her? She added a bit more makeup to allow for the dimness of the evening light.

Her thoughts turned to Nina, who had laughed delightedly when Katie told her about the invitation to the admiral's party. "Are you kidding me?" she had asked.

"No. I was just as surprised as you. I naturally thought he would already have invited someone. Surely he would have arranged a date long before this, don't you think?"

Nina started to say something, then she just shrugged enigmatically and turned her attention to wiping the counters.

The sound of the doorbell interrupted her reverie, and Katie went down to answer it.

As she hurried to meet her date, Katie's heart thudded in anticipation. She unlocked and opened the screen, and Camden's gaze swept her admiringly. He gave a deep sigh. "For a minute there I was afraid I would be greeted by the first Katie . . . the one I encountered the day I met you."

Katie laughed. "Thanks to Nina, I think the old Katie has disappeared."

"That's a relief." He opened the box he was carrying under his arm, and carefully lifted out an exquisite, creamy lei. He gently placed it over her shoulders.

"Ginger blossoms," Katie murmured, inhaling the exotic fragrance of the cool flowers nestled against her throat. "How did you know that was my favorite?"

"Just a lucky guess. Are you ready to go?"

"Yes, I'll get my things." She picked up her small purse and the filmy scarf which would protect her shoulders if the air conditioning was too cold. It was a soft blend of three shades of blue, including the azure blue of her dress. As they left, she carefully checked the heavy outer door to make sure it was locked.

They drove down the narrow street, passing bead and trinket stands which never closed, small private homes, a gift shop, and a grocery store. As they headed toward the beach road, more upscale tourist shops appeared, and lining the beach, the lavish hotels which were the base of the island's economy.

Katie glanced at Camden's profile, so strong and appealing. "I guess you'll be pretty busy tonight with all the details of the party."

"Not really. There were other people on the committee to see to some of the details. Actually, there's no reason I can't relax and enjoy the party, now that I have that extraordinary cake." He turned and gave her a quick appreciative grin.

So, she mused, *my analysis of his last-minute invitation had been wrong.* She gave him a penetrating look. "Do most of the officers take dates to something like this?"

"Yes, usually. I'm still congratulating myself that you were available."

"I wouldn't have been if it wasn't for Nina. She is really remarkable. I can't thank you enough for steering her my way. You know, she's really quite intelligent. Much more so than any of the other people I've hired."

"Yes, I noticed that, too. She just found herself in a desperate situation and made the best of it. I think it shows strength of character."

"I hope she doesn't leave. I'd be so disappointed if I lost her."

"Don't worry. She won't quit. I happen to know she is very fond of you."

"Have you known her long?"

"No, I just got to know her for the first time the other day. I saw her working at the Club, but never had a conversation with her, then . . ." He hesitated, but decided not to go on. "Oh well, never mind."

As they drove along the coastal highway, a red sun hovered just above the water, spreading coral rays that capped the foam of the surf. It was a dazzling sight that enticed Katie's imagination. "Wouldn't you love to be swimming in that?"

"Mmmm, I can almost feel the warm water. Why don't we do that next Sunday, when I have a little time off?"

"That would be great."

They were approaching the Officer's Club. Camden turned in and drove up to the front door, where a young valet took his car and parked it. People were arriving in a constant stream.

Camden spoke to several officers, and they exchanged introductions. It appeared to be one of those large, festive occasions, where the evening consisted of good food, lots of superficial chit-chat, and a speech that one hoped would be mercifully short.

Apparently Camden was in Admiral Bronfman's good graces, because when they were introduced, Katie was aware that he took special notice of her. "Well, well," he said in that gruff tone he used for anyone less important than the President of the United States, "when did you meet this attractive young lady?"

Camden smiled at her proudly. "This happens to be Katie, of Katie's Cakes. She's the one who made your retirement cake."

Admiral Bronfman looked her over appreciatively. "Hmmm. I can hardly wait to try it. You have quite a reputation around here, young lady."

Katie smiled. "I hope you like it."

"I'm sure I will."

They mingled and exchanged small talk with numerous other guests straight through the cocktail hour. Katie was aware of a blur of officers and their dates, beautifully dressed, all wearing leis. The fragrance at times seemed quite overwhelming.

She was relieved when Camden suggested they step outside for a breath of fresh air. The light breeze ruffled her hair and brought the cooling, refreshing scent of the sea.

Camden stood close to her, and far enough away from another couple so that they couldn't hear. She felt his arm around her, and his face near hers. "You're quite stunning tonight," he murmured, and lightly nuzzled her ear.

She felt an overwhelming desire for him to kiss her, and started to turn her face toward his, when she saw the lights inside blink. "Oh, I guess it's time to go in to dinner."

He managed a quick kiss on her cheek before they turned to go back into the banquet room.

When they were seated at their table, she turned to Camden. "Your admiral doesn't seem so ferocious to me."

"Maybe not to you, but believe me, he was on good behavior tonight. He eats junior officers alive."

"It's strange you would say that. I had the distinct impression he likes you."

"Maybe . . ." He didn't finish, since the waiter brought their salads.

Katie managed a bit of conversation with the older woman sitting next to her. She was married to one of the senior officers, who had been stationed in Hawaii for many years. She explained that her husband would be retiring next year, and she had no idea where they would live when they returned to the mainland. "Personally, I would just as soon stay here, but Henry is determined to go back so we can be closer to our children."

By the time they finished their salads, the entrees were served. They had steak, a mélange of vegetables, and duchess potatoes. Katie sampled it and thought it was quite well prepared. She turned to Camden. "You know, this is better than I expected. I didn't know military food was this good."

"They do a fine job here. I think it's actually better sometimes when it's cooked in a large quantity."

"You may be right. I must admit I'm a

bit nervous—I do hope the admiral likes his cake."

"Don't worry. He'll love it."

As the plates were being removed, the guests were introduced, beginning with the wives and families of the senior officers. Suddenly, Katie heard her name from the podium. ". . . and our final introduction, Katie Weston of Katie's Cakes, who made Admiral Bronfman's beautiful retirement cake. Stand up, Katie!"

Smiling and flushed, Katie stood briefly, amidst a flurry of polite applause. "I wasn't expecting that," she told Camden as she sat back down.

"The Admiral must have mentioned it to him. I hope you don't mind."

"Not at all. It's good advertising."

Katie felt relaxed driving back to her house with Camden. The party was fun, and everyone congratulated her on the delicious cake. Admiral Bronfman had loved it.

Camden was especially pleased. "See, you saved my life. If it hadn't been for you I'd be sitting in the brig in irons at this very moment."

"Really, Camden. You shouldn't give that nice old Admiral Bronfman such a bad time." She took a deep breath of the fragrant cool air. "Isn't it a gorgeous night? Now that the sun has gone down it's absolutely perfect."

He turned on some music. "Couldn't you sit a little closer? It's lonesome way over here."

She scooted over toward him until she felt his arm slide around her shoulders. There was little conversation the rest of the way. Perhaps, she thought, he was feeling as conscious of her nearness as she was of his.

He walked her to the door when they arrived at her house. "Thanks for going to the party with me. I enjoyed showing you off."

"I should thank *you*. It was a delightful party, and it was nice to meet some of your friends."

He gave her a hug and a warm kiss. "I'll call you about that swim next week." And then he was gone.

Katie locked the door behind her, switched on the light, and checked her answering machine. A contented smile was still on her lips as she went into the kitchen.

"Oooooh!" An anguished cry escaped from her lips as soon as she flicked on the light. Dangerous shards of glass from a broken window lay sparkling like diamonds on the floor, reflecting the moonlight from the unprotected window.

Chapter Four

When Nina showed up for work Monday morning, Katie had already called someone to replace the window. In the meantime, she had managed to find a big enough piece of cardboard to cover the window opening.

They exchanged the usual how-was-your-weekend pleasantries before Nina went into the kitchen. Her reaction to the cardboard-covered window was just what Katie had expected. Nina did a double take, then gasped. "What happened to the window?"

Katie explained what she found Saturday night when she came in from her date.

"I'm afraid someone wants to get rid of me."

"Now, now," Nina said soothingly. "Let's not jump to conclusions. "Haven't I seen a young boy playing around outside? Did you find a ball in here anywhere?"

"I'd love to think it was something innocent, but no, I didn't find a ball."

Nina went outside and Katie followed. There were signs of trampled grass under the window. She turned to Katie. "See, most of the glass has been knocked out. He could have clambered in and retrieved his ball, then run off, probably scared to death of being caught."

Katie nodded. "I suppose that's possible." They returned to the kitchen. "I have to get busy. There's no point in wasting time playing detective. Let me know if you see the kid anywhere, and I'll try to have a word with him."

Nina was so sensible, Katie mused later after she had left. She had been so unnerved by the broken window that she'd imagined all sorts of dire things. She even checked her valuables, in case there had been a robbery. There was no sign that anyone had been anywhere in the house except for the evidence right there in the kitchen.

The glass man had arrived in mid-afternoon, quickly replacing the window. "We get lots of these," he told her. "I'd say about ninety percent of them are broken by kids playing ball." He smiled. "I broke my share of them when I was a kid. My dad always made me face the music and apologize to the neighbors. And I had to pay for it out of my allowance, too."

Katie didn't bother to tell him she had not received any apologies or offers to pay for the repair.

Later that evening, as she was sitting outside enjoying the sunset and the cool breeze, her nerves were soothed by the flamboyant blossoms of her bougainvillea. She had sent a picture of it to her parents. "This is why I couldn't leave Honolulu," she had scribbled underneath it. Of course they understood.

The ringing of her portable phone on the small table beside her startled her out of her reverie. It was Camden calling from the club. "Nina just told me what happened. Do you need any help?"

"No, but thanks for calling. Everything has been taken care of. The window glass is already replaced."

"How do you think it happened?"

"I'm not sure. Nina thinks it was a kid who plays around here occasionally. He's about ten, I'd guess. She thinks he broke the window with a ball, then scrambled in through the window to retrieve it. I hope that's all it was. At first I thought it was part of the pattern of my long string of assistants who quit."

She admired Camden's reaction. "I get off about noon tomorrow. We need to know exactly what happened. I'll find that boy and talk to him."

"Oh, I hate to put you to all that trouble."

"Not at all. We'll get to the bottom of it right away," he said firmly.

"All right." She loved his decisiveness.

"We can make plans for our swimming date then," he said. "You're still planning on that, aren't you?"

"You bet. I'm looking forward to it."

The next morning, Katie got an early

start on her work in the kitchen so she would have plenty of time to spend with Camden.

"Keep an eye out for that boy," she told Nina. "Camden wants to talk to him."

"Now we're getting somewhere. You can bet he'll get to the bottom of it."

"You think so?"

"Absolutely. He has a way of getting things done."

Katie nodded. He certainly did—of that she was sure. "I think I'll fix a plate of sandwiches and a pitcher of lemonade, since he's coming by around noon."

"Good idea. You go ahead with what you're doing, and I'll make the sandwiches." Nina opened the refrigerator. "When you get through there, you might want to go upstairs and primp a little."

Katie laughed. "Really, Nina, if I didn't know better I'd think you were some kind of a matchmaker."

"Just thinking of your best interests." She stopped in the middle of her sandwich-making to answer the phone. Katie heard her go through all the questions involved in taking an order. When she finally finished, she turned to Katie.

"Another wedding cake. Romance is in the air."

Katie shook her head and glanced at the ceiling. Nina was a hopeless romantic.

It was a little after twelve when Camden stuck his head in the door. "Is this the scene of the crime?"

"I'm afraid so." Katie pointed to the window. "That's the one that was broken . . . shattered, actually."

"You should have called me. I would have come right over and helped you clean up."

"That's too kind of you. I was frightened at first, but after I checked the rest of the house and saw that nothing was missing, I calmed down a bit."

"That was pretty risky. What would you have done if you had found someone in the house?"

"I guess I would have died of fright."

"See—that's why you should have called me."

"How about a sandwich before we start our detective work?"

"Great. I'm starving."

She put the plate of sandwiches on the

table, and poured lemonade for both of them.

He bit into one of them hungrily. "Mmmm, these are just like the ones they make at the club. They're the best in town."

"That must be because Nina made them." She called out to Nina, "Would you like a sandwich?"

"No, thanks." Nina called back. "I ate one while I was making them."

He took a big sip of lemonade. "Tell me about this boy. What time do you usually see him around?"

Katie thought a moment. "I guess usually in the middle of the afternoon. Nina thinks he did it, then scrambled in to get his ball and ran away."

"Sounds reasonable to me," Camden said.

"I'm not so sure. I don't think he'd be hanging around my property when I'm not home."

"Do you want to bet?"

"Sure. If we find out he did it, I'll cook you a dinner. If not, dinner's on you."

"That's a deal."

After lunch they decided to split up.

"You try that little bakery over there," Camden suggested, "and I'll talk to the woman at the mom and pop grocery store."

A young man in a white apron worked behind the counter at the bakery. He finished ringing up the sale of some cinnamon rolls.

Katie smiled at him. "My, that smells good. I'll bet you sell a lot of those."

"Yes, what can I get for you?"

"I'm Katie Weston. You know, of Katie's Cakes. I'd like half a dozen of those chocolate chip cookies."

He put them in a white bag and Katie paid for them. "Incidentally, I was wondering if you had noticed a young boy about ten years old who comes around in the afternoons sometimes?"

"I guess you mean the King Shus' grandson."

"Do you happen to know his name?"

"I think it's Jimmy."

"They're the people who own the grocery store, aren't they?"

"That's right." Two customers came in, and he turned his attention to them.

Katie left and headed for the grocery

store, just as Camden came out. He made a thumbs-up sign. "Got it," he said.

"I know. The boy is their grandson. The man at the bakery told me."

"Yeah, and they're not too friendly. Don't hold your breath until the boy comes around to apologize."

"Why not?"

"I don't know, but I do know this much: the boy lives with his grandparents."

"I wonder where his parents are."

Camden spoke with determination. "Well, I intend to talk to him."

They spent another hour strolling around the neighborhood, talking with as many people as they could. A middle-aged woman sat patiently under the shade of a big banyan tree, watching hopefully as an occasional tourist stopped to finger the necklaces at her bead stand.

"Come on," Camden said. "I'll buy you a necklace."

Katie looked at several necklaces, holding them up against her face. "I can't make up my mind," she said. "What do you think?"

"I don't know." Camden turned to the

woman. "They all look good on her, don't they?"

"Yes. Very beautiful lady."

"Do you come here every day?"

"Yes. This is my business." She reached under her table. "Here, this one is pretty."

Katie held up the coral colored beads. It was a cheap imitation of real coral. "Yes, I like this color."

Camden continued his interaction with the woman. "You have a nice selection here. By the way, I don't suppose you've noticed a young boy about ten who lives around here somewhere? He dropped something in her yard the other day, and she wants to return it."

"Oh, that's Jimmy King Shu. He lives with his grandparents behind the grocery store."

"Really. What happened to his parents?"

The woman turned away and didn't meet his gaze. She shrugged. "Maybe you should ask him." She turned to Katie and held up the coral necklace. "You want this one? I make you a special price."

"How much?"

"Five dollars. Real bargain."

Camden held out three dollars. "This is the best I can do."

The woman took the money and put the necklace in a small sack. "All right. It's yours."

They walked back towards Katie's house. "You're a tough customer," she said.

"She's a tough salesman. Those necklaces don't cost her more than fifty cents. How would you like to make 500% profit on every cake?"

Katie laughed. "All right. I just didn't want to take advantage of her."

They were almost to the grocery store when they both spied him at once, ambling along, dribbling a basketball. Camden called out to him. "Hey, Jimmy. Could I have a word with you?"

The boy looked up, startled, then dashed off in the opposite direction.

Camden overtook him easily. "What's your hurry? I just wanted to chat a bit."

"I'm not supposed to talk to strangers."

"That's all right. I'm not a stranger. I'm a friend of your neighbor's."

Katie caught up with them. "You know, Jimmy, I was just wondering if you had seen anyone around my house Saturday night."

He gave her a look of alarm and refused to answer. "I have to go home. My grandmother is expecting me."

"Okay. We'll walk back with you. My friend here thinks someone might have accidentally broken my window with a ball. Do you suppose that is what happened?"

His eyes were big, a startling Irish blue in his Asian face, but still there was innocence in them. "I don't know who broke your window."

It was not a very promising start, but still Katie held out hope that she could befriend the boy. He was cute, and she liked children.

Camden exchanged a look with her. "I guess we had better talk to your grandmother."

By this time they'd arrived at the grocery store, and the grandmother stood at the door. She shooed him into the house without a word, then spoke to Katie. "What do you want with my grandson?"

"Someone broke a window at my house

Saturday night. I thought he might have seen someone around. Maybe you could help me."

The grandmother's expression was cold. "I saw no one." Without another word, she turned and went back into her store.

Camden and Katie looked at each other, then turned back toward her house. There was a lump in Katie's throat. "*Now* do you believe I have a problem?"

"Yes. If Jimmy broke your window, why would he be so afraid to admit it?"

Katie didn't speak until they were inside her door. "Oh, Camden..." She couldn't continue because her voice broke.

He gently turned her toward him and drew her close. "I promise we'll get to the bottom of this, Katie." He tipped her face up toward his and kissed her tenderly.

His mouth felt warm against hers and she closed her eyes to shut out everything else. This was the kiss she had longed for ever since they stood together outside the Admiral's retirement party.

The air between them was charged with

electricity. She felt his warmth against her, and for the first time, her awful sense of foreboding dissolved in the security of this man's embrace.

Chapter Five

The first sound Katie heard when she awoke the next morning were the birds chirping outside her window. She stretched and smiled, content in her flimsy little home. A fresh breeze, redolent of oleander, wafted in through the curtains covering her open window.

She put on a light cotton robe and went into the kitchen to get some breakfast. The weather was too perfect to stay indoors, so she took a cup of coffee, a bowl of cereal, and half a papaya out to the little café table on the small patio outside her kitchen door.

There she settled in the soft morning

sun to eat her breakfast. She squeezed a little lime juice on her papaya and savored a luscious bite while she planned her day. It would be busy as usual, but she could still enjoy this quiet time by herself.

She looked out over the driveway where her van was parked, and beyond to her neighbor's backyard where their dog lay sleeping. That's when she saw Jimmy King Shu sticking his head around the corner of her house.

"Good morning, Jimmy."

"Hello. I sneaked out while my grandmother wasn't looking."

"Have you had breakfast? Would you like some papaya?"

"No, I have to get back, or I'll be in trouble." His eyes were downcast. He shuffled his feet, and finally spoke in a low voice. "I know what happened to your window."

"You do?"

He still didn't meet her gaze, but continued to hang back in an embarrassed way. "I broke it with my basketball." His eyes were big as he finally looked at her. "I'm real sorry. It was an accident."

"I see. Does your grandmother know?"

"No, ma'am. I'd really get in bad trouble if she did."

Katie waited, hoping he would offer to pay for it. "I'm glad you told me the truth, Jimmy. That was the right thing to do."

"I wish I could pay for it, but I don't get an allowance. My grandmother says I have everything I need, and I don't need an allowance, too."

"I'm surprised about that, Jimmy. Do your friends at school get allowances?"

"Yes, ma'am. My best friend, Kyle, gets five dollars a week. He also has a basketball hoop in his driveway, and a bicycle. My grandmother won't let me go over to his house after school, though."

Katie was thoughtful for a moment. "I'll tell you what, Jimmy. You could pay for that window by doing some chores for me for a few weeks. How about that?"

He brightened. "Sure. What would you like me to do?"

"How about taking my trash out every morning, and sweeping off my porch?"

"I could do that. If I left for school a little bit early my grandmother wouldn't know the difference."

She could tell he was feeling better

now. He actually grinned at her. "I was afraid you'd be really mad at me."

"Of course not. Accidents happen. I understand, and I'm glad you told me the truth about it. Here," she held open the door, "I'll show you where to empty the trash."

"I was born in this house," he said, glancing around the utility room. "Grandmother says my mother's spirit is still here."

"Do you remember your mother?"

"No, I was just a baby when she died."

"I'm sorry, Jimmy. That's very sad."

"I see her picture every day, but I've never seen my dad's picture."

"You haven't? That's odd."

"My grandmother won't talk about him. I snoop around and try to find something about him every chance I get, but there isn't anything there."

"I'm sure you're very curious. I would be."

"I don't suppose you found anything here, did you?"

"No. This house was rented to other people until I bought it, so I'm sure it was cleaned out long before I moved in."

Katie showed him where to deposit the trash outside and when they came back in, he noticed the ladder that led up to the attic from the utility room. "What's up there?"

"That's the attic. I've never been up there, but I'm sure they cleaned it out before they sold it." She hadn't thought about it before, but now she wondered why she never bothered to check it out. Climbing that steep ladder and pushing open the overhead door probably hadn't seemed worth the effort.

"I'll do it tomorrow when I come over to do my chores," he promised. "Right now I better hurry and sweep off the porch before my grandmother misses me."

She watched as he left. *That poor kid,* she thought, *being held back by well-meaning grandparents who know nothing about what young boys need.*

She went in and dressed, then started her first cake.

Nina showed up at the usual time, looking bright and chipper. " 'Morning Katie. I see you already have a cake in the oven."

"Yes. I wanted to get an early start. Camden is coming for lunch."

Nina beamed. "Can't stay away from you a minute, can he?" She took the lid off the trash can, preparing to take the trash out. "What's this? Did you already take the trash out? You know that's my job."

"Sorry, Nina, but I'm afraid you've been supplanted for a while." Katie told her about Jimmy King Shu.

"That little scamp. I knew he did it. Well, at least he owned up to it. I'm glad you let him earn his share of the damage. It's a good lesson for him."

"He's like a prisoner over there. They won't let him do anything. It's a wonder he hasn't gotten into more trouble."

"I wish you could talk to them, but I guess that would be very awkward."

"Next to impossible."

By the time Camden showed up for lunch, Katie had finished a beautiful cake for a teenager's birthday. It was encircled with pink rosebuds, and little tendrils of green ivy gracefully fell over the edges. A tiara was centered on the top, as her father always called her Princess.

Nina admired it extravagently. "It's one of your best. I'd have thought I'd died and gone to heaven if I ever got a cake like that when I was her age."

"Me, too, but these days young people take all this for granted."

"Oh, here comes Camden."

Katie hurried in to open the door for him. "Glad you could stop by."

"Yeah. How's it going?"

"Just great. I had an interesting visitor this morning."

"Oh, who?"

"Jimmy King Shu came over and made a confession."

"Is that so? I knew he did it."

He leaned down and gave her a warm kiss. "Now, how about that home cooked dinner you owe me?"

"I don't know what I was thinking, making a dumb bet like that with you. How about a week from Sunday?"

"Okay, it's a date. It will give me something to look forward to. A fellow needs a good home cooked meal every once in a while."

They talked about Jimmy while they ate their lunch. "He's so cute, Camden. It took a lot of courage for him to come over and confess to breaking my window. I wish you could have been here to see him."

"That shows character, all right. Maybe his grandparents aren't doing such a bad job after all."

"No, he's being held down too much, I can tell. I've been thinking about it, and I've decided to go over and try to talk to them again. What do I have to lose?"

"Well, when you look at it that way, you're right. Do you think he knows anything about his parents?"

"Not much. He knows his mother died when he was a baby, and her picture is displayed in the house, but he is intensely curious about his father and they've never told Jimmy a thing about him. It would be interesting to find out just exactly what happened."

They finished their meal, and went outside to take a little walk together. They could see Nina watching at the door as they walked hand in hand down the path. "She seems awfully pleased about us," Katie said. "Have you noticed?"

"Yes, I think she must be quite a romantic."

They hadn't walked more than half a mile when they turned back toward the house. Clouds were gathering, and they knew a brief tropical shower would unleash itself at any minute.

"I have to get back," Camden said, once they reached the porch. He leaned down and gave her a kiss. "I'll see you Sunday."

She watched as he drove off. What did she ever do without him?

It was almost four o'clock when Katie finished making her deliveries. As she drove home, she made a decision. She would pay a visit to Jimmy's grandparents.

First she stopped in the bakery for some more brownies, then she went over to the grocery store. Jimmy saw her and gave her a look of concern. She winked and put her fingers to her lips, to reassure him that she wasn't there to tell on him.

His grandmother turned from checking out a customer and smiled at Jimmy.

Katie held out her bakery bag. "I just

got some brownies at the bakery, Jimmy. Would you like one?"

He looked at his grandmother hopefully, and she nodded. He took one and thanked her politely.

Katie noticed a small picture of a beautiful young woman on the counter next to the cash register. "Is that Jimmy's mother?"

Mrs. King Shu's face clouded over. She turned to Jimmy. "Go out and play."

Katie offered him another brownie, which he took, and ran out the door.

His grandmother picked up the picture and looked at it lovingly. "Yes, that is our daughter, Mara."

As she spoke, her husband came into the room from the back. He appeared frail and gentle. It was clear that his wife was the disciplinarian in the family. "Did I hear Jimmy come in?"

"Yes, he went out to play. I was visiting with our neighbor, Katie Weston."

Mr. King Shu nodded to Katie solemnly. "Perhaps you could offer Miss Weston some tea."

"Would you care to join me, Miss Weston?"

"Thank you, and please call me Katie." She followed Mrs. King Shu through the back door into their small living room, pausing to slip off her shoes and don the soft slippers kept there for guests. There, a large picture of their daughter was displayed on a side table.

Mrs. King Shu offered Katie a seat next to a round table. She poured tea with grace and dignity, every movement deliberate.

Katie waited while Mrs. King Shu sipped her tea, then set her cup down. She had to remind herself to sip her tea slowly and carefully in the Japanese manner. At length, she spoke. "I presume Jimmy never knew his mother."

There was a painful silence until Mrs. King Shu spoke sadly. "She became sick after the boy's father left, and died of pneumonia." Another long silence. "We are certain she died of a broken heart."

Katie spoke softly. "How very sad. And Jimmy's father?"

"He didn't know his father, either. He left—returned to the mainland before Jimmy was born. We've often wondered if he even knew she was expecting."

Mrs. King Shu poured more tea for both of them. She set the teapot down with an unsteady hand and took another sip of tea. "Mara waited and waited, but he never returned. It was too much for her."

Katie felt her eyes glaze over with tears, and her hand reached out to enfold hers. "I am so sorry. I had no idea."

Mrs. King Shu rose. Apparently their tea was over. She spoke in a low, earnest voice. "You must be very careful, Katie. You could get your heart broken. That's all I can say."

Katie thanked her and walked out quickly. She couldn't wait to tell Camden what she had learned. As she walked back toward her house, a light tropical shower intensified the fragrance of the plumeria trees that lined the walkway.

Even so, she was so preoccupied with thoughts of her visit with Mrs. King Shu Katie hardly noticed the shower. What an odd experience, getting close to the woman who had stayed so aloof ever since she had moved into her house. Now she had many more unanswered questions to pique her curiosity.

Chapter Six

Katie was just finishing her coffee when Jimmy arrived, carrying his ever-present basketball and dressed for school. He knocked on the back door, and immediately got busy emptying the trash. "You didn't say anything about my accident to my grandmother, did you?"

"Not a word. That's our secret."

He returned the trash container to its place in the utility room, then looked up at the attic door. "Is it okay if I go look around up there now?"

"Sure, go ahead, but be careful." She handed him a flashlight. "Stick this inside your jeans. You'll need both hands."

He scrambled up the steep ladder like a little monkey and pushed the door open. It was no problem at all for him to get through the opening. Soon he started back down, holding a box a little larger than a stationery box, which he handed down to Katie.

"Is that all you found?"

"No. There was a broken chair and some old faded curtains."

He reached the bottom and pushed the ladder back up to the ceiling.

Katie opened the box. It held a naval yearbook and some snapshots. "It looks like the previous tenants were a military couple."

"Yeah. I guess I'd better sweep off the porch and get going."

He looked disappointed. Katie wondered if he had really expected to find some clue to the whereabouts of his father. "Don't be discouraged, Jimmy. Something may turn up yet."

He finished sweeping and scooped up his basketball.

Katie smiled. "You must be a pretty good player, aren't you?"

"Yes, I never miss a free throw, but one

of the guys, Mike Kampala, says I'm too short to play basketball."

"Maybe he's just jealous."

"That's what I think. I fixed him, though. His sister worked here and I told him this house was haunted."

Katie remembered the name. "Was Estelle Kampala his sister?"

"Yeah, also Mary Kampala and their cousin Jean Manoa." He grinned. "They all quit."

Katie gave a big sigh of relief. "So *you* were the cause of all my employment troubles!" There was no point in chastising him. He'd meant no harm. "Scoot along now so you won't be late," she urged.

Wednesdays weren't usually very busy, but Katie had cake orders for two events. She finished decorating the pink merry-go-round cake for a little girl's birthday party in the afternoon, and called Nina to come look.

"Didn't this turn out well? I should pay *them* to make these, it's such fun."

Nina nodded. "It's one of your best. What else are you doing today?"

"I'm making a cake for the Officers'

Wives' Panhellenic Tea. They're incredibly fussy, so I'd better have a steady hand."

Just then the telephone rang, and Nina went to answer it. Katie had already started the panhellenic cake when Nina stuck her head in. Her eyes twinkled merrily. "You're wanted on the phone. He says it's urgent."

Katie wiped off her hands and went to the phone. Camden's voice gave her a familiar surge of pleasure. "Hi. What's up? Nina said it was urgent."

"Yes, I have to buy a birthday present for my mother this afternoon, and I need your help."

"I wish I could, but I have to deliver a couple of cakes this afternoon."

"Katie, you don't know how urgent this is. I haven't the vaguest notion of what to get her. I always goof up, you have no idea. She'll open Gary's present and say, 'Oh, just what I wanted, a beautiful Japanese porcelain. I'll put it on the mantel.' Then she'll open mine and say, 'What's this? A potholder set. How interesting.' "

In spite of herself, Katie giggled. "I can see you do have a problem, but . . ."

"Couldn't Nina deliver those cakes?"

"Well, all right. Come by about two."

"Thanks. You're a lifesaver, and a doll."

She sighed and returned to her kitchen. "He's done it again, Nina. He talked me into going with him to buy his mother a birthday present this afternoon. Would you deliver these cakes for me?"

"Sure, don't worry."

"I don't know how he does it, but he has this way of persuading me to do things when I know I shouldn't."

Nina agreed. "I think it's a talent. No one can turn him down."

Katie hadn't thought of it as a compliment, but knowing how Nina felt about him, it didn't surprise her that she had taken it that way.

While the panhellenic cake was baking, she placed the birthday cake in its plastic holder and secured it in the delivery van. How had she ever managed without Nina? Actually, not very well, she had to admit. Since she could never repay Camden for Nina, she rationalized, she really shouldn't turn him down when he asked her for a favor.

As she worked on the cake, she thought about their upcoming shopping expedition. Where should they go? Liberty House always came to mind, since it had long been the choice for bridal registries and Christmas shopping sprees for Hawaii's upper-middle-class shoppers.

She slid the cake into the oven and set the timer. Camden's mother should have something unique that she couldn't buy at just any big department store.

By the time Katie had showered and dressed, Nina was on her way with the two cakes, and she had an excellent suggestion for Camden's mother's birthday present.

When he arrived, she met him at the door, ready to go.

"How can you cook all morning, then look like you just stepped out of the beauty shop?" he asked, admiration beaming from his eyes.

She laughed. "I'm still trying to overcome my bad first impression."

"Where do you think we should go? I'm really a desperate man."

"Now just relax," she said soothingly. "This isn't going to be an ordeal. Why don't we try the little silk shop over by the Halekalaini?"

"That's the nice hotel with the orchid in the bottom of the swimming pool, isn't it? I've been there."

"Yes, it's just possible we might find the perfect gift there."

As they drove, she explained how Jimmy was the cause of her employees leaving.

He laughed. "So you worried for nothing. Nobody wants you out of the neighborhood, after all."

"I could have wrung his little neck, but I was too relieved to criticize him."

Once they reached the silk shop, Katie found she had another problem. It took superhuman restraint to keep her mind on why they were there. She had never seen so many stunning outfits in one place in her life. She wanted to stop and try on everything she saw.

You're here to find a present for Camden's mother and that's all, she told herself sternly. *Don't forget—you owe a ton of money and you can't afford a thing.*

"Look, Camden. How about one of these darling pillows?"

"Yeah, that might be just the thing."

Katie stood back and admired the silk pillows. They had flowers painted on the front, and were signed by the artist in the corner. "What color would go in your mother's living room?"

"Uh . . . I don't know. I guess I never thought about it."

"Well, you said she had a blue and white collection. How about one of these white ones? I like this one, with the green foliage and the peach colored hibiscus. Or would you rather have the dendrobium orchids?"

"Mmmm, I think she'd like that one, the hibiscus." Camden made the purchase, then they left. And as they were leaving, he said, "That was painless."

"I hope you're feeling better now. She may put your brother's Japanese porcelain on the mantel, but she'll put your silk pillow on the living room sofa."

"I knew I could count on you," he said with a big grin. "It's still only the middle of the afternoon. How about stopping for some ice cream?"

"That would be perfect, but we'd better hurry—I think one of those little clouds is about to unleash a shower on us."

They ducked into a nearby ice cream shop and ordered ice cream cones.

Katie didn't hesitate. "I can't resist anything with macadamia nuts."

Camden nodded. "And I can't resist anything chocolate. You know, Katie, even if I hadn't had to buy a present for my mother, I don't think I could have made it through 'til Sunday without seeing you."

She smiled. "I'm glad you needed the help. It wasn't very difficult to persuade me to turn over my deliveries to Nina, was it?"

"Not very." He reached over and squeezed her hand. Outside, the rain battered on the roof in a quick, hard shower.

"We just made it, didn't we?" she said.

"Yeah. It's kind of cozy being in here together, with the rain coming down hard outside."

"I've been dying to tell you what I did after you left yesterday."

"Oh, what?"

"Let me put it this way: guess who I had tea with yesterday?"

"Not Jimmy's grandmother!"

"That's right. Actually, Mr. King Shu suggested it. Oh Camden, it was so sad. She told me about how her daughter died right after Jimmy was born. She died of pneumonia, but Mrs. King Shu said she actually died of a broken heart."

"That is sad. What about his father?"

"Well, that's even sadder. He deserted her, went back to the mainland and just left her high and dry. They're not even sure he knew she was pregnant."

"Maybe that's why she refuses to talk to Jimmy about him—she doesn't want to say anything bad about his father to him."

"I was so touched I didn't even ask her what I wanted to know, and I just couldn't bring myself to suggest she give Jimmy more freedom."

As they talked, the rain stopped as quickly as it had started, and the sun broke through the clouds. "I guess we had better go," Katie said. "I should get back to the house."

Camden dropped her off at her back door, after leaning over to give her a quick kiss. "Thanks loads. I'll see you Sunday."

Chapter Seven

Katie hadn't expected to meet Camden's brother any time soon, if ever; however, a phone call on Wednesday told her Gary would be in Honolulu for the weekend. "I'm anxious for you to meet him. Could you have dinner with us at the Officer's Club Saturday night?"

"I'd love to. Is this an unexpected visit?"

"No, he's on his way to the mainland for a two week vacation."

"Good. I'll look forward to meeting him. Why don't we postpone our Sunday date until next week, since I'm sure you'll want to spend more time with your brother."

69

"Yes, maybe we'll go sailing or something."

A knowing smile wreathed Nina's face when Katie told her about her plans to meet Camden's brother Saturday. "That's a very good sign, you know."

"It is?"

"Oh yes. It means he's proud of you and wants to show you off to his big brother."

"I hadn't thought of it that way."

Nina nodded wisely. "Siblings are very competitive, you know."

"Is that so? I never had a sibling."

Katie was determined to live up to Camden's pride in her. She dressed with extra care for their date on Saturday night. Since blue was her best color, she wore a becoming silk sheath, which accentuated her figure and matched her eyes. Camden's admiration was apparent when he saw her. "Every time I see you, I think you couldn't be more beautiful. You are such a knockout in that dress."

"Thanks. I'm glad you like it."

"Gary is meeting us at the club."

"Tell me about him so I won't be entirely clueless. If he's anything like you, I'm sure I'll like him."

"Well, actually, we're very different. Sometimes I think he must work at it. He's surprisingly laid back and casual. I don't know how he ever got through basic training without ending up in irons."

"It doesn't sound like he would fit into the military mode very well."

"I'm sure he had problems, but he's so likeable he gets away with things that would get most people in trouble." He drove down the coastal road, heading for the Officer's Club.

The sight of the ocean with the sun setting behind it always gave Katie a thrill. It was different every time, changing from salmon pink to magenta, sparkling with the whitecaps that rippled in on the waves.

Boats were sailing smoothly in the distance, expensive yachts cruising along the water with their lights twinkling; and even this late, surfers were coming in behind the boats, their brown bodies shining.

"Wouldn't you love to be swimming out there?" She could almost feel the warmth of the water, the way it would be when they swam together, and the way Camden's chest would slide against her as they lolled in the water close together. She cast a furtive glance at him, so earnestly concentrating on his driving, and a surge of desire swept through her.

He nodded. "Would I ever."

"Will I like Gary?"

"I think so. Just because he is different from me, doesn't mean he isn't thoroughly likeable. He does have a good sense of humor, and he knows how to have fun. Yes, I believe you will like him . . . but not too much, I hope."

She laughed. "Don't worry. I'm sure that won't happen."

He pulled the car into the parking lot and glanced at his watch. "We're right on time, so he probably won't be here yet. Promptness isn't one of Gary's strong points."

They went in and took a seat at the bar. "There's no point in going in to a table until he gets here. We might have to wait too long to order. Would you care for something to drink?"

"Just sparkling water." The bar was already full. They took the last two seats, and looked around. It was a typical Saturday night scene. Quite a few officers were there with dates, some with their families, and parents who were visiting.

It was already noisy, and they had to raise their voices to talk to each other. Camden glanced at his watch again. "Don't worry. He'll be here pretty soon."

"I'm in no rush." She knew better than to expect everyone to be prompt. It was one of her virtues, and one she admired in others, but a lot of people just couldn't manage to get anywhere on time. She wondered why that was.

Finally, after Camden had looked at his watch for the fourth time, he glanced at the doorway, and there was his brother.

Katie followed his gaze. Gary was shorter than Camden by several inches, but nevertheless quite handsome. A warm smile brightened his features when he caught sight of his brother, and he hurried over toward them.

They grasped hands warmly, and slapped each other fondly on the back, chuckling with pleasure.

Camden introduced Gary to Katie, and

she found his greeting mixed with curiosity and envy . . . or was it exasperation? "Camden, you sly fox, how in the world do you do it? How is it you always have the most beautiful woman in the room on your arm?"

The look on Camden's face was one of slight annoyance. "Don't exaggerate. You make it sound like I hop from one woman to another."

"Let's just say you're resilient."

Katie watched this exchange with some discomfort, to say nothing of curiosity. Resilient? What was he talking about?

She spoke hastily. "Let's go in and get a table. I'm starving."

Camden agreed. "Me too. Come on, Gary, we'll order you a drink at the table."

After ordering their drinks, the men both decided on steaks without even looking at the menu. Katie gave it a quick glance, and settled on mahimahi.

"I'm glad you're going home," Camden told his brother. "I've been wondering how Mom and Dad are doing since they retired."

"Me, too. I didn't think they would ever

leave Hawaii. You know Mom really loved it here."

"Well, it's a big decision. Katie's parents retired and moved back last year."

Katie nodded. "They're very happy, but it was a difficult decision to leave the islands."

Their drinks arrived, and Gary took a sip, then turned to Camden. "Pardon my curiosity, but how did you two meet?"

"Oh, it was just one of those things." He told the whole story, then added, "If you had seen her that day, there is no way you would have asked her out for a date."

Gary looked her over with a raised eyebrow. "I find that hard to believe."

"But I didn't recognize her the day she delivered the cake. That's when I chased after her and asked her for a date before she could get away."

"But what ever happened to . . ."

Camden interrupted with a quick subject change. "I sent Mom a birthday present the other day. I'm sure you didn't forget, did you?"

"No, of course not. I thought she would like a Japanese porcelain. I found an especially beautiful vase at one of their exclusive shops."

"Sounds lovely," Camden murmured complacently, nudging Katie with his foot.

Their food was served shortly, and the men seemed quite pleased with their steaks. "How's your fish, Katie?" Camden asked.

"Excellent. Mahimahi is my favorite island fish." They talked about the military, and their prospects for the future. "I have a few more years in Japan," Gary said, "then I'll end up back on the mainland, but I'm not sure where yet. Maybe Annapolis. I think I'd like that."

They finished their meal and the two brothers made plans to spend Sunday together. They invited Katie to join them for sailing in the afternoon, but she declined. "I really think you two should have that time to yourselves. I'll get back with you later," she told Camden.

As he drove her home, she told him she liked his brother. "You're right, you and Gary are not much alike, but I can see there is genuine affection between you two. He seems to admire you a great deal."

"I think you have that backward—*I* admire *him*. I'm just the little brother."

"No, I can see he has a great deal of respect for you." She gave him an impish grin. "What was all that about your always having the most beautiful woman in the room?"

Camden laughed. "Oh, he was exaggerating. That was just his way of complimenting you." He put his arm around her. "How about sitting a little closer?"

She scooted over next to him. "Is this better? I don't want to interfere with your driving."

"You know, Gary was right. You were the most beautiful woman in the room tonight, but then you always are."

"Never mind the flattery. You'll turn my head." She leaned against his shoulder, feeling the warmth of his body through the thin silk of her dress.

Once they reached her house, Camden parked in front, and they went inside. As soon as they entered the house, Katie's stomach tightened, and she felt the familiar apprehension. "I'd better check to see if everything is all right, then I'll fix us some coffee."

She dreaded finding another broken window in the kitchen, or who knows what else? But when she checked the house, she found everything was just as she left it. She turned to Camden. "It looks fine. Let's have some coffee."

They took their cups into the living room, where Katie turned on some music.

Camden indicated a spot next to him on the sofa. "Sit here beside me and relax. How are you and your friend Jimmy getting along?"

"Fine. He hasn't missed a morning yet, comes by right on time and gets his chores done."

"Did you say he found something in the attic?"

"Yes. I've been too busy to go through it. Let me go get it." She went to the utility room and brought back the box, which she opened. "Jimmy was so disappointed. He had hoped to find a clue to his father hidden up there."

"See." She handed him the yearbook. "It must have belonged to the previous tenants."

Camden took it. "I don't know. Look at the date, 1991. That's when Gary was here."

Katie was thoughtful. "Wait. Wouldn't that be the year Jimmy was born?"

"See?" Camden showed her Gary's picture, and continued leafing through it. "Here's J. J. They were great friends. I wonder what ever became of him? I'd like to show this to Gary. Would you mind if I took it, to show him? I'll return it right away."

She took a sip of her coffee. "Not at all. Do you think there's a chance Gary could help us find Jimmy's father?"

"I wish, but we don't even know his name."

"What do you suppose Mrs. King Shu's reaction would be if I asked her?"

He finished his coffee. "I think it would alarm her. If she thought we were trying to find him, she would worry that he would try to take Jimmy away from them."

"I guess I had better hold off for a while. More coffee?"

"No, just move over closer." He nuzzled her face with little kisses. "Just relax."

She closed her eyes, and gave herself over to the delightful caresses that accompanied his kisses. How could she possibly worry at a time like this?

His lips touched her eyelids with little tender kisses, and she felt their warmth as they circled around her hairline. At last, they touched firmly on her mouth.

She returned his kisses because there was no way she could resist the feeling inside her. The magic of the night, the warm fragrance of the ginger blossoms nearby, and the soothing rhythms of the soft music engulfed them in an irresistible cocoon.

Chapter Eight

Katie planned her week carefully. She didn't want the last-minute hassle of getting the order ready *and* dressing for the party at the Naval Officer's Club. This would be like most weeks, in that it started slowly and ended very busily.

She saw Jimmy off to school after he finished his chores. He was becoming increasingly restless, and it worried Katie.

After breakfast, she did some paperwork until Nina arrived. As usual, Nina was in a good mood. They chatted while they worked. "Incidentally," Nina said, "I heard that Camden is moving up in rank.

Isn't that exciting? He's so smart, there's no telling how far he can go."

Katie smiled at Nina's enthusiasm. "It's great news. He has asked me to attend the ceremony and the party afterwards."

"Wonderful. I knew he would. You'll have a great time."

"Camden is coming over for lunch today. He wants to discuss the cake for their party Saturday night."

"In that case, I'll just make up a plate of sandwiches, unless you need me to do something else. Would that be okay?"

Katie smiled at her. "Camden loves your sandwiches. That would be just great. How about making a pitcher of lemonade, too?"

"Of course, I'll take care of that for you."

"That would be wonderful, Nina. You're sure you don't mind?"

"I'd love to. You need to get organized for the week."

"Yes, I'm trying to plan everything so I won't be swamped at the end of the week like I am sometimes."

* * *

Camden was in a good mood when he arrived. "Admiral Miller asked me to arrange for another cake like the one you did for Admiral Bronfman's retirement party. He thought that one was just too good to be true."

"Oh, really? How nice."

"All you need to do is to change the insignia on the top. You can do that, can't you?"

"Of course." She leafed through her catalog. "How about this?" She pointed to an anchor with a captain's insignia on each corner of the square cake.

"That should be fine. What's for lunch?"

"Sandwiches, fruit, chips, and lemonade. Same old thing. You know, you didn't have to come all the way over here just to tell me to make the same cake with a different insignia."

"I know. I just wanted an excuse to come over and see you." He grinned confidently.

As they munched on sandwiches, Katie told him about her latest conversation with Jimmy. "I really wanted to tell him that that yearbook might hold a clue to his father, but I just told him not to get discouraged, that something might turn up. He needs just any little scrap of hope at this point."

"Have you looked at the pictures that were in the box?"

"No, I haven't had a minute. As soon as we finish eating I'll get them. Can you spare the time?"

"Yes, I'm very curious."

After lunch, they took the box of pictures and spread them out on the sofa. There were snapshots of naval officers and their dates out on picnics and other kinds of outings.

Camden held one out to her. "Look at this. Doesn't she look Asian?"

"Yes, kind of like Jimmy's mother. It could be her, but I can't be sure just from that little snapshot."

"That's J. J. with her."

"Gary's friend?"

"Yes. Wouldn't it be something if he turned out to be Jimmy's father?"

"I'll say, but the chances are remote. You know what a melting pot Hawaii is. Some of the people are mixtures of three or four different races." Katie sighed.

"Find out from Gary if J. J. ever went out with Mara King Shu. It's a small chance, but it's all we have to go on. I'd give anything if we help Jimmy."

"I'm pretty sure he's still visiting my parents. I'll e-mail him as soon as I get back."

When they finished lunch, they took a little walk, which had become a routine by then.

"Nina said to tell you goodbye. She thinks you're the best. I can't imagine how you two got to be such good friends. I don't believe you ever told me."

"Oh, really? It just sort of happened. Listen, I can't stay long, but I wanted to tell you about the latest."

The smell of the ocean filled the air. They walked hand in hand.

"Yes. What's going on at the base? Has Admiral Bronfman left yet?"

"Well, yes and no. He'll be at the party Saturday night, as an honored guest. He will be retired here in Hawaii, which has always been his plan."

"How do you like his successor?"

"Oh, Admiral Miller will be just fine. He's had plenty of time to prepare for the transition. He's a good officer, well-liked by the men. I don't anticipate any problems."

As they strolled along, Katie realized that she had failed once again to find out how Camden and Nina had become such good friends.

Camden called a few days later to tell her he had received an e-mail from his father saying Gary had gone to Santa Barbara to visit friends for a few days. He promised to relay Camden's e-mail to his brother when he returned.

"So, unfortunately I have no news that would shed light on Jimmy's father yet. But I'm sure looking forward to Saturday."

"Me, too. I'm sure it will be a lovely affair. I'll deliver the cake before lunch."

"Good, I'll be watching for you."

On Saturday, Katie was delighted to wake up to an utterly perfect day. Her spirits soared at the thought of seeing Camden promoted, and all the festivities that accompanied the event.

She delivered the cake before lunch.

There were already signs of the preparations for the afternoon's special event.

As usual, she hoped to get a glimpse of Camden. He stuck his head out of the dining room as she walked in. "Hi. I was hoping to see you." He glanced at the cake. "Perfect. I can hardly wait to taste it."

He walked out to the car with her. "I'll pick you up at a quarter to three. It's going to be a nice ceremony."

"I'm sure it is. I'm looking forward to it." She could tell by the way he was looking at her that he wanted to kiss her.

He glanced back at the building, then quickly leaned down and kissed her. "I couldn't resist," he said boyishly.

She climbed into her van and started the motor. "I'll see you this afternoon," she said. Then she drove off as he stood and watched until she was out of sight.

Her thoughts were warm and tender as she savored the feel of his kiss. Once more, she realized she might be the luckiest woman alive.

Later, the sun was bright overhead, and a warm breeze softened the tropical heat.

Katie wore a pale blue dress which

Camden had never seen. She supposed he wouldn't notice even if she wore the same thing every time she saw him, but she had a special feeling about today's event, and she wanted to look special, too.

She watched out the window as his car pulled up. What was it about uniforms? There was a little ache in her heart as she watched him walk up to her entrance. She pushed open the door. "Hi, I'm ready."

He just stared at her without a word. Finally, he put his arm around her and hugged her. "I give up. I didn't think you could top the way you looked at Admiral Bronfman's retirement party, but just look at you. An ordinary guy like me doesn't have a chance."

She grinned. "You're exaggerating. You always do that."

"Not at all. I'll be afraid to let you out of my sight."

As he drove down the familiar road, Katie relaxed, not thinking of anything except the moment. "I'm glad you like your new commanding officer. I'm sure some of them can be tough occasionally."

"Yes, there are plenty of those, but we've been lucky with the last two. I'm sorry to see Admiral Bronfman leave. He was an especially nice guy."

"Do you usually have the same musicians for these parties?"

"Yes, they're the best at what they do. The popular classics are good for dancing, and everyone seems to like them."

"I suppose there will be a lot of families there to watch their officers promoted to a higher grade."

"Yes. I hope it won't be too boring for you. These affairs are built around years and years of tradition. Each officer must be honored individually as he receives his upgrade."

"I won't be bored at all. I'm looking forward to it."

"Well, at least the party afterwards will be fun."

There wasn't much time after they arrived before the ceremony began. Katie found a seat in the large auditorium. As she expected, she was surrounded by the parents and other family members of the officers being honored.

The ceremony was called to order and began with a prayer by the chaplain. After that, a brief speech by the Admiral described the training and hard work behind these well-deserved promotions. Finally, the men were called up one by one to receive their insignias, followed by a handshake from the admiral.

When Camden's name was called, Katie's heart swelled with pride to see him walk up to the front, so straight and tall. He appeared to be one of the youngest officers to become a captain that day.

After the ceremony ended they left the auditorium and went on to the dinner. Katie congratulated Camden. "I'm sure you were one of the youngest officers to become a captain. I was so proud of you."

He beamed at her words of praise. She supposed there was a bit of sibling rivalry behind his determination to get ahead and keep up with his brother.

There were hors d'oeuvres before dinner, and they mingled with some of the same friends they had chatted with at Admiral Bronfman's party. It was a warm evening, and the doors and windows were open to let the ocean breeze circulate throughout the crowded room.

At dinner, they enjoyed an ample meal of roast beef, garlic mashed potatoes, and assorted vegetables. Katie enjoyed the food, but as she told Camden, "If I ate like this too often I'd look like one of those women who wear only mumus."

"We work this off in no time at all around here," he assured her.

Admiral Bronfman made a point of exchanging pleasantries with them after the dinner was over. The tables were pushed back along the sides of the room, and the musicians took their places and tuned up for the dance.

As the music started, Camden asked her to dance. They were well-matched on the dance floor. He was a smooth dancer, but not a show off. After the first set, they sat down and refreshed themselves with cold drinks.

So far, it has been a delightful party, Katie thought. At that moment, the music started again. This time a familiar old classic. The words ran through Katie's head as the music player . . . *It's very clear . . . our love is here to stay. Not for a year . . . forever and a day.* It was one of her favorites.

She glanced at Camden, about to suggest they join the others on the dance floor, when she noticed a strange expression on his face. She followed his gaze, and just inside the door she saw the object of his attention.

The most stunning creature she had ever seen stood just inside the door. She was tall and very slender. Her shiny, shoulder-length blond hair set off the white form-fitting dress, which accentuated her perfect figure.

Katie looked at Camden and saw that he looked as if he had seen a ghost. When she looked back at the blond, Katie saw that she was making her way across the floor, heading straight for Camden.

Once she reached them, she held both hands out to Camden. "They're playing our song. Won't you dance with me?"

Camden's face turned from white to red. He stood and turned to Katie. "This is Alicia Bronfman, Katie. Alicia, this is Katie Weston, my date."

Could this be Admiral Bronfman's daughter? Katie looked over at him, and he was watching them, frowning with displeasure.

She acknowledged the introduction politely, then stood, and with a voice that sounded like that of a perfect stranger, she asked Camden to take her home. "I've developed a dreadful headache, I'm afraid."

Camden asked Alicia to excuse them, and they left, with a good part of the room watching their every move.

Once they were in Camden's car, Katie broke the strained silence. "I take it you were surprised by the appearance of this Alicia person?"

"You might say that. To tell you the truth, I never thought I'd see her again."

He drove out onto the oceanfront road, and the only sound was the whirr of the tires on the road. Finally Katie spoke. "Would you care to tell me who she is, Camden? I presume she is Admiral Bronfman's daughter."

"Yes. We used to go out together, before she went back to the mainland." There was a long silence. "I might as well tell you everything. Alicia and I were engaged. Shortly before I met you, she left me a letter saying it had all been a mistake, and she was going back to California."

"I see. Then you met me on the rebound. It's an old story, isn't it? I guess I was pretty naive, although I did wonder why such an attractive man was still unattached."

"Don't get the wrong idea, Katie. I was hurt when she dumped me. I didn't expect to find anyone else for a long time. You were so different from Alicia . . . so real and down-to-earth, I fell like a ton of bricks."

He reached over and took her hand. "Nothing has changed between us. I admit I was shocked to see Alicia so unexpectedly, but I no longer have any interest in her. Now that I'm with you, I realize Alicia and I would have been a big mistake."

During the fifteen-minute drive back, there were frequent long silences, then questions would arise in Katie's mind. "How long were you with Alicia?"

"About a year. I didn't meet her until she came over to join her parents. She had been working in a law office since she graduated from college, but she wanted the experience of living in Hawaii."

"I see. I thought Admiral Bronfman had

a special fondness for you . . . now I know why."

"I have a great deal of respect for him. It's true he liked me, and I'm sure he would have been pleased to have me as a son-in-law."

"How did he feel about Alicia breaking your engagement and going back to the mainland?"

"He was actually quite angry about it, and even said his daughter always had been fickle. Apparently he was right about that."

When they reached her house, Camden offered to go in with her and check to see that everything was all right.

She hesitated. "Are you sure you don't just want to say goodbye now?"

He put his arm around her and held her close. "Don't even think such a thing. I should have told you about Alicia before now, but she's history, and as far as I was concerned, she had nothing to do with us."

Katie sighed, wanting to believe him, yet feeling terribly vulnerable.

As Katie unlocked the door they saw that everything was just as she left it.

"Thanks for coming in with me." She walked him to the front door, where he took her in his arms. "Katie, I never want to be the cause of any unhappiness for you. You do believe there is nothing between Alicia and me anymore, don't you?"

She wanted to believe that more than anything else in the world. "Yes, I believe you, Camden."

His kisses were warm and sweet as he held her close and kissed her over and over again.

By the time he finally released her, she was convinced that he wanted her as much as she wanted him. With her heart pounding, she said good night.

"I'll call you tomorrow," he promised, and he turned and walked into the night.

Chapter Nine

Nina's voice echoed the alarm that Katie felt. "You mean Alicia Bronfman is back?"

"Not only is she back, but she's after Camden. I wish you had told me about her."

"My word!" Nina shook her head in disbelief. "I wanted to, but I figured it was Camden's place to tell you."

"Of course it was; I'm not criticizing you. He should have told me long ago. I felt like such a dummy when she showed up. It seems I was the last person in Honolulu to know about her."

They were working in the kitchen, making a fancy anniversary cake which had been ordered last week. Nina checked the recipe and set the oven. "I'll never forget the night Alicia dumped Camden. Of course, I didn't know her, but Camden came in the bar occasionally with his friends."

"Well, it was such a coincidence. My husband had just walked out on me . . . left me flat with a ton of debt. For a few minutes there I didn't care whether I lived or died. Then, I just figured I'd manage some how."

She poured herself a cup of coffee and took a sip. "I don't like to think of all that." Then she continued. "When Camden came in, he looked like he had been kicked in the stomach. I couldn't help but feel concerned. Even though it was none of my business, I asked him what happened."

"Some people would have told me to get lost, but Camden is a real gentleman. He didn't say much. 'My fiancée just dumped me,' I believe was what he said.

"I told him I could sympathize . . . that the same thing had just happened to me, only it was my husband. By the time I got through telling him that my husband and his fiancée weren't worth ruining our lives over, he had to agree with me. I told him the real love of his life was out there somewhere, and I just knew he'd find her soon."

Katie smiled. "You're something, Nina. It's no wonder Camden is so fond of you."

"Now go on about Alicia. Did she change her mind about wanting someone else?"

"Apparently so. All I know is, Camden says he knows now they would be all wrong together, and he still loves me. I admit I've had a few worried moments, but I do believe he means it."

Nina nodded. "He's smart enough to know you're just what he needs. You hang in there, and don't let that woman take him away from you."

That was so like Nina, Katie couldn't help smiling. "I don't intend to."

He had been over Sunday, worried that Katie was upset by Alicia's untimely appearance. He reassured her over and over that he still loved her, and wanted nothing to do with Alicia.

* * *

In the meantime, Katie wanted to keep the lines of communication open between herself and Mrs. King Shu. She invited the older woman over for tea, knowing it would be polite to reciprocate.

Promptly at four the following day, Katie was pleased to see Mrs. King Shu approaching her house. She was such a tiny woman, she took doll-like steps. Katie opened the door and welcomed her into her living room.

"Come in. I'm so glad you could join me." She indicated a seat near the coffee table, set with a pot of tea and a plate of cookies and sandwiches. "How are you?"

"Fine, thank you. And you?"

"Just fine. And how is Jimmy today?"

"Very boisterous, as usual."

Katie smiled at the description, which certainly fit her grandson. She carefully poured two cups of tea in her best teacups. "Help yourself to some refreshments."

Mrs. King Shu very deliberately took a lemon slice and a small teaspoon of sugar and stirred her tea. She gracefully sipped it, then placed the cup back on the saucer.

Katie sipped her tea slowly, then replaced her cup. "I love children. When I see him in the neighborhood I stop and chat with him. He does resemble your daughter."

At the mention of her daughter, Mrs. King Shu's eyes were downcast, and she hesitated a long time before speaking. "Yes, I agree."

"Does he also resemble his father? I imagine he's curious about him." Katie held her breath.

Another sip of tea preceded her answer. "I'm afraid so. But that subject is closed at our house."

"I understand. Forgive me for bringing it up." She offered the plate of refreshments to Mrs. King Shu, and she took a cookie.

Katie poured more hot tea into their cups.

The little Japanese lady took another graceful sip of tea after sweetening and stirring it. "Jimmy needs to keep his mind on his school work. As long as he studies after school every afternoon, he will not have time to get into trouble."

Mrs. King Shu finished her tea, then rose and thanked Katie graciously. "It is good to be in this house. I can almost feel the presence of our Mara."

Katie smiled at the thought. She held the door for her and watched as she headed for her store. But she closed the door, a thought occurred to her: she had once again missed the chance to suggest to Mrs. King Shu that Jimmy needed more freedom to be with his friends.

With the arrival of the weekend, it finally was time for the beach date Katie and Camden had been planning for so long.

They had been driving for about twenty minutes. The highway followed along the ocean, and the natural beauty surpassed anything Katie could remember seeing anywhere else in the world. Tropical flowers grew in masses along the roadside, like weeds do back on the mainland, she observed.

The water was three shades of blue, coming together in cascades of white foam. Although she wasn't an artist, she wished she was so she could paint it. Then she became more realistic. "I wish I had thought to bring my camera."

As they drove, Katie told him about having Mrs. King Shu over for tea. "Oh, she was very gracious. I took a chance and said something about how Jimmy was probably very curious about his father."

Camden's eyebrows went up in surprise. "How did she react to that?"

"About like you would expect. She said that was a closed subject in their house." She ignored Camden's snort, and continued. "She thinks that he can't get in trouble as long as he is kept busy studying after school."

Camden's reaction to that remark was just what she would expect. "That lady doesn't know much about raising little boys, does she?"

"No. I'll be glad when you hear from Gary. I hope he can help us find some clue to Jimmy's father."

"We should hear soon. I'll call you just as soon as I know anything." Camden turned on the air conditioning. "Looks like it's going to be a hot day."

"Yes, I'm already feeling parched," Katie agreed. She reached for the bottled water she had brought along. "How about a drink of water?" She passed it over to

Camden, who tipped it up and took a big swig.

"Thanks, that helps a lot."

"You know, Camden, no matter how long I live here, I'll enjoy this island just as much as any tourist."

"Yeah, me, too."

Katie felt a sense of calm and well-being as they drove.

Soon Camden slowed the car. "We're coming to the place where the surfers congregate. The waves are better here. Let's park and watch for a while, shall we?"

He pulled up in a sheltered spot overlooking the water.

Some of the surfers were little more than children, but they had grown up in the water. They were utterly fearless, their brown young bodies glistening in the sun.

"It must take a lot of courage to do that," Katie said.

Camden disagreed. "At that age they don't know the meaning of fear."

He shifted his position and changed the subject. "Speaking of nerve, it must have taken quite a bit to stay here and go into business on your own after your parents left the islands."

She shrugged. "I'm not sure it was so much a matter of nerve as it was innocence. In the first place, I didn't really think my parents would leave when Dad retired. It kind of caught me off guard. There wasn't much time to make the decision, and I just kind of fell into it.

"I really loved this place, and I just couldn't bear to leave it. I didn't realize how difficult having your own business could be."

"You managed to pick it up quickly enough," he said.

"Making the cakes was the easy part, the fun part," she said. "It was running a business that almost sank me."

He slipped his arm around her and squeezed her shoulders. "You know, I really admire your courage."

She sighed with pleasure at the warm sensation. His surreptitious kiss was natural and relaxed. She straightened before long. "I thought we were going for a swim."

He groaned. "Must we? I like things the way they are." Nevertheless, he started the car, and slowly drove down the road until they came to a place where the waves were calmer.

The water lapped gently at the beach in a quiet little cove. Out in the distance, where the waves came in, a few other swimmers could be seen. "Perfect," she said, as he pulled his car off the road and parked. "I can't wait."

She yanked off the shirt and shorts she had worn over her swimsuit, and ran down to the water. Turning, she called out a challenge. "I'll race you!"

Camden overtook her in a few long sprints. "Hah, you can't beat me," he called, laughing as he charged ahead. In the water, he swam with powerful strokes, as she watched in amazement. This wasn't fair—he swam like an Olympic gold medal swimmer.

As she watched, he swam out past the others, then rode a wave back in. Treading water, she waited until he came back to her, laughing at her look of chagrin. "Where did you learn to swim like that?" she demanded.

"I was on the UCLA swim team. Do you still want to race?"

"No, smarty. I just want to enjoy the feel of this water. It's like liquid silk, so warm and smooth."

She felt his arms encircle her. "Yes," he said, "since you put it that way, I have to agree." He nuzzled a quick kiss on her cheek before she broke away and swam out, with long, smooth strokes. She was a good swimmer, and she hadn't enjoyed a swim so much since she was a child and her grandparents had taken her to the lake at their summer home.

After they finished their swim, they spread out a beach towel and Camden brought out a basket of sandwiches. "Nina made these for us, as you probably suspected." He took a big bite of his sandwich.

"What made you decide to make a career in the military?" She asked as she opened a soda.

"That was Gary's influence. By the time I finished college, he had been in practically every country in the world. I envied him being able to see so much. At that time, I had hardly been out of L.A."

When they finished eating, Camden picked up everything and put the remains back in his car. "You don't have to rush back, do you?"

"No. It's awfully nice here. Why don't we relax and get a little sun before we return?"

"That's just what I had in mind."

They stretched out on their beach towels and Katie fished out her suntan lotion. "I'm so fair I have to use this stuff," she said, smoothing it on her face and body.

He volunteered to do her back, and it felt so good, she almost went to sleep. "Thanks," she murmured. "Do you want me to do you?"

"I hate that stuff, but I guess it's the only way I could get you to rub my back for me."

She chuckled. "Turn over."

He practically purred as she slathered the lotion slowly over his entire back. "Mmmm . . . don't stop."

"I have to. The suntan lotion is all gone."

She stretched out comfortably and let the warmth of the sun seep into her. As she lay there, almost asleep, she thought of their first meeting, so unpromising. How did they ever get this far? Perhaps it was just meant to be. She was far too sleepy to try to figure it out.

There was no sound from Camden. Apparently he was asleep, too. The distinctive smell of the ocean, full of kelp and brine, filled the air around them.

Finally, Katie felt like she was getting too hot. She punched Camden. "I'm afraid we're going to get a bad sunburn if we stay any longer."

"What?" He rolled over and blinked his eyes. "I was really out of it."

"I know. So was I." She noticed he was already bright pink. "I think we had better go."

With that, they shook out their towels and climbed into Camden's car. As they drove out onto the highway, Katie's laughter peeled into the late afternoon air.

"We're a charming sight now, aren't we?" she said, once her laughter had subsided. "Two slightly pink people, greased up with suntan oil and topped off with sand."

"I know. A shower is definitely in order."

"I haven't forgotten I owe you a dinner," she said.

"I'd love that."

"Shall we make it Sunday evening?"

"That sounds good. I'll call you before then."

As they approached the house, she gathered her things together. "I had fun," she said.

"Me, too. Let me help you in with those things." He took her beach bag, while she carried her wet towel and dry clothes.

Inside, she dropped her things on to the entrance floor, and wondered if Alicia ever let him see her in such an unglamorous condition.

He turned her toward him and held her tight, as if he had read her mind. "I like everything about you . . . more than you'll ever know." His kiss smoothed away every last doubt that tried to surface, and she relaxed in his arms.

Chapter Ten

Jimmy seemed restless and preoccupied when he came to empty the trash and sweep the porch Monday morning. He had very little to say, and Katie worried that something was wrong.

"Is everything okay, Jimmy? You're awfully quiet."

"Yeah, I guess," he muttered, banging down the top of the trash container.

"Have you and your grandmother had words?"

He turned his back and took out the broom, slamming the closet door as hard as he could. Finally, he spoke to Katie,

111

sounding like a teakettle about to whistle.

"My grandmother is driving me crazy. All she wants me to do is study, study, study. How can you keep studying something all the time if you already know it? I could do that school work in my sleep."

"Hmm, I can see you have a problem. Have you told her how you feel?"

"Oh, she doesn't pay any attention to what I say. If I could find my dad, I'd go live with him."

"Now, Jimmy, you mustn't think like that. We haven't been able to find him, and your grandparents love you and have done the best they know how. Maybe you could talk to them some more."

"Yeah, yeah. Maybe. I've got to go now." He put the broom back in the closet and slammed the door again, then he was out the door, holding his basketball under one arm and his books in the other.

A call came from Camden on Monday night. His voice was filled with excitement. "I just received an e-mail from Gary. J. J. *was* married to Mara King Shu—he *is* Jimmy's father!"

Katie gasped. "That's wonderful!"

"Yes, but I'm afraid this is good and bad news. He hasn't been able to find out anything about J. J."

"How disappointing. I thought maybe there would be military records, or something."

"I know. To quote Gary, 'it was just as if he had dropped from the face of the earth'."

Katie's sigh was audible. "We're at a dead end, aren't we?"

"Yes, unless we can come up with some other way to find him. But at least we know Jimmy's father's name . . . that's something."

There were other things on Katie's mind that night which bothered her even more. She had told Nina that morning that Alicia was still in Honolulu.

Nina looked alarmed. "Are you sure?"

"Yes, I asked Camden. She's still here, looking for a job, and they're in touch."

"I don't like it," Nina said. "She's out to win him back."

"I know."

"But I don't really think she'll have any luck. I just wouldn't bring her name up again. Don't let him think you're worried."

"No, I won't. I probably shouldn't have brought it up yesterday, but I just had to know."

It was a difficult project for a Saturday wedding, but to Katie it was just another challenge. The bride, a wealthy California socialite, said that she wanted something different. She hated the idea of cutting the cake and feeding the groom the first piece.

Together, they discussed other options. The end result was that Katie would make little separate cupcakes. Five different floral designs would top each of them. They would then be displayed on tiers to resemble a huge cake. The guests would each receive one during the reception. It would take a lot of work to produce these ornate little cupcakes, but price was no object, so she made her plans accordingly.

Katie assembled her cupcake cake at the site, and stood back to photograph it. Once it was put together on the tiered stand, it looked like a huge cake, completely covered with flowers. She would certainly add the picture to her catalog, although there was little likelihood it would be ordered again.

The bride was thrilled when she saw it, and that pleased Katie immensely. The wedding photographer would take pictures of it, and there was also a newspaper photographer covering the wedding because of the prominence of the bride. All in all, it had been a triumph.

Katie gloated as she drove back home. Now her thoughts turned to the gourmet meal she would produce for Camden the next day. Other less pleasant thoughts tried to intrude, but she fought them back. She and Camden had fallen into the habit of Sunday night dates because, like tonight, her business often made it impossible for them to go out on Saturday nights.

When visions of Camden out with Alicia tried to intrude, Katie turned the music up loud and refused to think about it. Instead, she told herself Nina was right: he would much prefer to be with her.

* * *

The soft lavender haze that bathes the world in the moments between sunset and moonlight cast its spell on Katie and Camden. They sat outside at her little round table next to the bougainvillea, sipping their drinks and nibbling hors d'oeuvres.

Their heads were almost touching as they chatted in low voices. Camden's words made Katie's spirits soar. He tried to sound pitiful. "Why did I have to fall for someone who works on Saturday nights? I was so sad and lonely last night, watching my friends leave for their big Saturday night dates."

"Please, you're breaking my heart. I'm trying to make it up to you tonight."

"Well, all right." He sounded like a pouty little boy. "By the way, how did you manage with all those fancy cupcakes?"

"It was a smash. The wedding will be in the Sunday paper, and I'll show you the picture I took of the cake later."

"Good, I knew you could pull it off."

"There is a lot of tension with a project like that. So much can go wrong."

When they finished their drinks, they went inside, and Katie filled their plates.

The rack of lamb was served with green peppercorn sauce, and sugar peas and roasted potato wedges accompanied the dish.

As Katie served them, she supposed Camden wouldn't care what the place settings looked like, but she enjoyed making her table a work of art when she entertained. It was set with deep blue place mats and napkins, white plates, and blue-stemmed glasses. Fuschia oleander blossoms centered the table, between blue and white candlesticks.

Katie felt lucky that Camden wasn't one of those steak and potato men who wouldn't eat anything the least bit interesting. He made a big fuss over the lamb, and she was glad she had made the effort.

They talked about the impossibility of finding J. J., who had disappeared without a trace for no reason they could possibly imagine. It was so sad to think of poor Jimmy, pining for his father, and endlessly searching for some scrap of news that would bring them together.

For dessert they had warm bread pudding with vanilla sauce, then they sat in the living room to have their coffee.

The rest of the evening would live in her memory for a long time. She put on some romantic music, carefully chosen from among her favorite CD's which she had collected over the years. Camden shared her love of music, and she could tell he responded to it the same way she did.

His kisses were ardent as he held her close, helping her to relax and enjoy these rare moments together. The warmth of his kisses sent messages of love she longed to believe were sincere. For the moment, she pushed everything else aside.

The week ended happily, but the days that followed brought unexpected problems and a desperate sense of urgency.

After mapping out the week's work with Nina, Katie felt confident she could win Camden back from the tentacles of Alicia once and for all. But for now she dismissed her rival from her mind, and kept her focus on business.

She was also concerned about Jimmy. He appeared to be on the verge of exploding that morning. How could she help him?

She hesitated to talk to Mrs. King Shu about him. Somehow she felt certain the elderly woman would resent it. There was something to be said for remaining on good terms with her—she might be in a better position to help Jimmy if she didn't clumsily spoil her relationship with his grandmother.

It was not until five o'clock that afternoon that the phone call came that sent tremors of worry through her. Mrs. King Shu's voice had tearful notes of panic in it. "I've called nearly everyone in the neighborhood, Katie. Jimmy didn't come home after school, and nobody has seen him."

Katie had feared something like this would happen, but she still wasn't prepared for it. She took a deep breath and tried to think how she could help. "Have you called any of his friends?"

There was a tremulous quality to Mrs. King Shu's voice. "I don't know any of his friends."

How strange, Katie thought. *Don't they ever talk?* "I'll see what I can do. Don't panic."

But Mrs. King Shu *was* panicked, there was no doubt about it. "If we don't find him by the time it gets dark, I'll have to call the police."

"All right. Let me make some phone calls, and I'll get back to you," Katie said, in as soothing a voice as she could muster.

She tried to gather her thoughts. There was Kyle, but she didn't know his last name. Then there was that other fellow, whose sister worked for her and quit. She did have that number.

Grabbing her address book, she looked up the number. There it was: Estelle Kampala. Jimmy had said her brother, Mike, told him he was too short to be a basketball player. Quickly, she tapped in the phone number. A girl answered, and she asked to speak to Mike. "Oh, he is at Kyle's playing basketball."

Katie leaned forward hopefully. "Oh. Would you happen to have his phone number?"

She held her breath as she tapped in the number and asked for Jimmy King Shu.

After a brief wait, Jimmy's voice came on the line. "This is Katie, Jimmy. Your grandmother called and she is worried to death because you didn't come home after school."

"Yeah, I was really mad. I guess I'm in bad trouble now, huh?"

"Just promise you'll go home right home now, and I'll talk to her and try to soften her up."

"Okay, Katie, but she'll probably kill me."

"Promise, Jimmy?"

"Okay, 'bye."

Katie called Mrs. King Shu. "Jimmy is on his way home now. I'd like to come by and talk to you."

"Oh, thank heavens! You have no idea how worried I was."

Katie rushed over to the store, and Mr. King Shu motioned toward the back. "She's expecting you."

"How can I thank you? Do sit down. I was just sitting here trying to think how I could punish him."

"That's why I came over," Katie explained. "I hope you will be more lenient with Jimmy. I'm terribly worried that the next time he defies you, it will be to disappear on a mission to find his father."

Mrs. King Shu's shock was almost palpable. "Why would he do that?"

"I might as well tell you. Jimmy is obsessed with finding his father."

"He has been very preoccupied lately. But I can tell you right now he will never find him."

"Why are you so sure?"

"He sent Mara a letter from California when he was sent there. He had been gone several weeks, and we tried to call him, but there was no way to reached him. In the letter he said he would always love her, but he could not return. He sent her enough money to pay for the house, and said not to try to find him, because he was changing his name."

Chapter Eleven

Camden groaned. "Changed his name? Now we'll never find him!"

Katie had called him as soon as she returned from the King Shus'. "That's just what Mrs. King Shu said. Why would he go to such lengths to disappear? I just don't understand it."

"Neither do I. We're really at a dead end now."

She told him the latest about Jimmy's failing to come home after school, and about their conversation.

"I wouldn't worry too much about a kid going home after school with a friend. That happens all the time."

"I know, but I'm so afraid he'll disappear on a mission to find his father."

"Let's hope he doesn't do that."

"I don't even want to think about that possibility."

Camden's voice was soothing. "Maybe we'll think of some way to find J. J., but right now I don't know how. We can talk about it when I see you for lunch."

"Yes. I'll see you tomorrow then."

Katie awoke to the sound of rain. The clouds had drifted in during the night, silently gathering overhead. Now the dawn brought a hard tropical downpour, which began the day with a soggy start.

She rose and dressed more carefully than she ordinarily would have to work in the kitchen, but there was good reason for it because Camden was coming for lunch. It had become a habit for them. She remembered once he had said he couldn't make it until the weekend without seeing her. She held that thought close. It buoyed her spirits at a time when she needed it.

This week she would have Saturday night free, and Camden had already told her he wanted to take her to a nice restaurant. She had a wedding cake to deliver by one o'clock Saturday, so this left her with plenty of time before he picked her up.

She was already at work in the kitchen when Nina arrived, cluck-clucking over the weather and shaking out her wet umbrella.

"What a day! Mercy, I thought the car would float right off the road. Why do you suppose we can't just have a nice, gentle shower without all this mess?"

"Quit your grumbling. It's going to be a great day. Camden's coming for lunch, and if you don't get greedy and eat your sandwich while you're making it, you can join us."

Nina's smile told her she had hit on the right note to improve her bad humor. "He can't stay away from you long, can he?"

"I hope not. He's taking me to a nice restaurant Saturday night, so I'm looking forward to that."

"I hope you know what a lucky lady you are."

"Oh, I do, Nina. I do."

The phone rang, and Nina went to take

an order while Katie busied herself starting a cake for a bridal shower.

The rain stopped as abruptly as it had started, and by the time Camden arrived, the sun was shining brightly.

"It's a steam bath out there," he said, "but at least it has stopped raining." He leaned down and gave Katie a big kiss on her forehead. "What's for lunch? Some of Nina's sandwiches, I hope."

"You guessed it. How come you're in such a good mood?"

"Well, that's because I just got some surprising news." He and Katie sat down at the table while Nina went in to get the lemonade out of the refrigerator.

"You are going to join us, aren't you?" Katie asked, as Nina poured their drinks.

"Are you sure? I don't want to intrude."

Camden motioned to the empty chair. "Oh, for heaven's sake, sit down. You're family."

Nina grinned. "Now I know how it feels to be adopted."

Katie helped herself to a sandwich, and passed them to Nina. "So what is your good news, Camden?"

"Gary is getting married. He's my

brother, Nina, and I swear to you I never thought he would take the plunge."

"Who is the lucky girl?" Katie asked, sipping her lemonade.

"She's a girl he went with before he left for Japan, and she left the base to go back to California and take a job there."

Katie thought about that. "And he didn't mention it when he was here?"

"Not a word. Actually, I don't think it occurred to him until he saw her again on this last leave."

"Oh, so that's it. She must have really gone to work on him."

"Yes, I think so." Camden turned to Nina. "I should explain we're both so surprised because, even though Gary is two years older than I, he is very laid back and irresponsible. In other words, he is a typical bachelor."

Nina thought about that. "And you're not?"

"Now Nina, I'm surprised you would ask me a question like that! Don't you know I'm just the opposite of Gary? I'm very compulsive and organized and responsible. I would be excellent husband material for some lucky girl."

Nina's response was more of a snort. "Hah!" She rose and went over to get the cookies, just as the telephone rang. "I'll get that." She put the cookies on the table and went to the desk to answer the phone.

Camden grinned mischievously. "I love to tease her." He rose. "Let's take some cookies and go for a walk."

Katie grabbed a couple of cookies and waved to Nina.

"You don't mind being out in this steamy heat, do you?" he asked.

" 'Course not. My kitchen gets pretty steamy at times, too, you know."

He took her free hand and they walked down toward the beach. "Let's see what the tourists are doing today."

They were doing what they always did, spread out on the damp sand, sunning, swimming, picnicking.

Katie looked up at Camden. "So, when is this wedding taking place?"

"Early next month. This girl is smart— she didn't want to wait long enough for Gary to change his mind."

"Where will it be? Surely not in Japan."

"No, I think they will go back to San Diego for the wedding, where our parents are, as well as the bride's. That means I'll have to make plans to get off. Incidentally, it would be a good time for you to meet my parents."

"Oh, really? You mean I will be invited to the wedding?"

"Certainly. Otherwise I'll kick and scream and refuse to go."

"Well, I do hope that won't be necessary."

Camden changed the subject. "What do you make of that strange business of Jimmy's father changing his name?"

"I don't know. According to Mrs. King Shu, he sent her enough money to pay for the house, and said that he loved her, but not to try to find him. That is really bizarre, isn't it?"

"Yes. Unless Gary knows something we don't know, we might as well forget it."

"Where does that leave poor Jimmy?"

"In the dark, as always. It's tough."

The rest of the week, Katie puzzled over what, if anything, she should tell Jimmy. She was tempted to show him the pictures of his father, but should she talk to Mrs. King Shu about it? Still undecided, she said nothing, hoping that he would be happy with the one day a week at Kyle's after school that his grandmother agreed to.

Camden had merely said they would have dinner at a place he thought she would like, so Katie didn't have much of an idea as to what she should wear. Now she waited patiently for him to pick her up. Since she didn't have a clue, she dressed in a black and white tropical print sheath she had fallen in love with several months ago. She knew it wasn't sensible to put things on lay-away, but sometimes that was the only way to afford something she really wanted.

Camden greeted her with a kiss, then held her at arm's length and gave her a low whistle. "You look simply smashing!" He said, in one of his funny accents that made her giggle.

He unlocked his car. "You're probably wondering if you're going to like this."

"It had occurred to me."

"Well, my guess is that you'll love it. It's brand new . . . It's called the Island Palms."

"I've heard about it."

"One of the guys at the base took his parents there and gave it rave reviews, so I figured it might be good enough for a famous gourmet chef like yourself."

She laughed. "I got all dressed up, then I thought 'if he's taking me to McDonald's, I'll kill him.'"

"Don't get snooty on me. I love McDonald's."

They drove out on the coastal road until they came to a driveway leading through a grove of palm trees. The restaurant was right on the water, so the tantalizing smell of the ocean filled the air as soon as they got out of the car.

Inside, the lights were dimmed and there was the sound of subdued conversation when they entered. Apparently Camden had made a reservation, so they were taken right to their table next to a window overlooking the water.

Katie looked out and remarked that it was just like being on a boat, except that there was no motion. "I already like this place before I've even tasted the food."

"It is nice. What are you in the mood for?"

"Some kind of fish. How about you?"

"Same here."

They looked over the menu. Finally, Katie made her decision. "I'm tempted by these prawns in lemon sauce with capers."

"I want something more substantial. I'm having the grilled mahimahi."

Since it had occurred to Katie that Alicia Bronfman had tried the same tactics as Gary's fiancée, she wondered if Camden had noticed the coincidence. Naturally, she was careful not to mention such a thing. "What is Gary's fiancée's name? I don't believe you mentioned it."

"Oh, didn't I? It's Eve Mallory."

"You like her?"

"Yes, she's a very nice person. I think she will be a good addition to the family."

"I suppose it will just be a small family wedding, won't it?"

"Don't ask me. That isn't my department."

Katie smiled at his innocence. "I just meant that there wouldn't be time to put on a large wedding. That can take up to a year of planning."

"That doesn't sound like anything Gary would sit still for."

Katie had ordered a butter lettuce salad with blue cheese, and when she tried it she couldn't restrain herself. "This is just the most wonderful salad I ever tasted." And so it went, all through the meal.

The Island Palms was everything she liked in a restaurant, from the romantic setting to the sumptious food.

On the way back, she sat very close to Camden, as they listened to soft music on his stereo. "You get an A+ for restaurant selection," she told him, snuggling closer as he put his arm around her.

"I liked it, too." He gave her shoulders a warm squeeze. "We'll have to come here again before it gets too popular."

Back at her house, Camden held her close. His face was warm against hers, and he murmured loving words as he kissed her over and over again.

Feelings of wonder and joy intermingled with the love awakened within her.

Words weren't necessary for her to know he shared her feelings. At last, he reluctantly said goodnight.

"I need to sleep on the problem of Jimmy's dad. Time is running out, so we need to get busy. Gary will be back pretty soon on his way to Japan. Once he leaves California, our chances of finding Jimmy's dad are practically non-existent. I'll call him and see if he knows of a friend or relative of J. J's we could contact."

She held the door as he left, and he gave her one last warm kiss. Nina was right—she was a very lucky lady.

Chapter Twelve

Before he even started his chores, Jimmy looked up at Katie with big, sad eyes. There was pain and resignation in his expression. "Katie, tell me the truth. Are we ever going to find my dad?"

"I don't know, Jimmy. Right now, we've come up against a blank wall. The problem is, he changed his name after he left on his last assignment. We don't even know if he is still alive."

Jimmy turned his back to hide the depth of his disappointment.

It was more than Katie could stand. "Forget the chores. Come sit here at the kitchen table, and I'll show you something."

She brought out the box containing the yearbook and loose pictures. "Do you remember when you brought this box down from the attic? I thought it belonged to the people who rented this house before I bought it, but I was wrong. It belonged to your parents."

His face brightened. "It did?"

"Yes. Camden realized it was dated the same year his brother was stationed here, which was also the same year you were born."

"Wow! Is my dad's picture in there?"

"Yes." She turned to the page in the yearbook where he was pictured. "Here he is."

Jimmy gazed at him for a long time. "He's a great looking guy."

"He certainly is, and I'll tell you something else. He was a close friend of Camden's brother, Gary. They called him J. J."

"Could Gary help me find him?"

"He's been trying to find him while he's in California, but he hasn't had any luck so far. I'll be honest with you, Jimmy.

When we found out from your grandmother that he had changed his name, we
knew our chances of finding him were
pretty remote. I'm terribly sorry."

"At least I know what he looked like."

She sifted through the photos. "Here's
a picture of him with your mother."

"Could I have one of these?"

"You can have them all. They belong to
you. Why don't you leave them here and
you can pick them up after school. In the
meantime, I'd better talk to your grandmother and tell her what I've been doing."

"Thanks, Katie." In a spontaneous ges-
ture, he threw his arms around her neck.

Katie tried to say "you're welcome" but
she was too choked up to speak.

"I guess I'd better run on to school. Can
I do my chores later?"

"You can skip them today, Jimmy. We
had more important business to take care
of."

After Jimmy was gone, Katie sat there
a long time. Had she done the right thing?
How would she ever know? It was done
now, and there was nothing left to do but
try to get Mrs. King Shu to understand

why she had done the equivalent of opening Pandora's box.

Nina burst in upon her thoughts. "I'm
afraid you're going to have to speak to
Jimmy about his chores. He's getting
pretty sloppy. That porch is a mess."

"I let him off the hook this morning,
Nina. Would you mind taking care of that
and the trash today?"

"Sure. No problem." She gave Katie a
closer look. "Something wrong?"

"Yes and no. I felt sorry for the poor kid
and let him see the pictures of his father.
Now I have to explain to his grandmother
what I've been up to. I hope she won't
take it the wrong way."

"Wow. No wonder you're so quiet. Well,
you had better get it over with. If you
don't it will just gnaw at you all day."

"I know. I'll have to do it in person, so
will you take care of things until I get
back?" She picked up the box of pictures
and the yearbook. "Wish me luck."

Nina's face held a look of real concern
as Katie left for the grocery store.

Mrs. King Shu looked tired. "My husband didn't sleep well last night," she explained. "I'm worried about his health."

Just then Mr. King Shu poked his head around the corner. "Hello, Katie." He frowned at his wife. "I'm fine. She always fusses over me."

Katie smiled at his response, then turned to Mrs. King Shu. "I need to talk to you. Could you spare a few minutes?"

"Certainly."

Her husband motioned toward the back. "You two run along. I'll keep an eye on things out here."

They went back to the living quarters, where Mrs. King Shu invited Katie to have a seat on the sofa.

Katie took a deep breath. "I hope you're not going to be upset with me. I don't quite know how things reached this stage, but I want to explain what I've done."

Mrs. King Shu eyed the box Katie held curiously. "Does this have anything to do with Jimmy?"

"Yes, everything. You see, the first time Jimmy came to my house, he told me he used to live there before his mother died. He said he had poked around all over your house looking for something that would give him a clue to his father."

"I didn't know that, but I guess I shouldn't be surprised."

Katie nodded. "He isn't any different from any other curious young boy. One day he pointed to my attic and asked if I had found anything up there. I told him I doubted that there was anything left, since it was probably cleaned out before I bought the house."

Now Mrs. King Shu was following her story with interest.

"He wanted to know if he could go up and look around. I saw no harm in it, and allowed him to climb up to the attic." She held out the box. "He came down carrying this."

Mrs. King Shu opened it, staring at the date on the yearbook. "Oh . . . my . . ."

"I didn't pay much attention, thinking it was left by the previous tenant. Then I showed it to Camden, and he picked up on it right away. That was the year his brother, Gary, was on the base here. He and J. J. were close friends."

Mrs. King Shu was staring at J. J.'s picture in the yearbook.

"Those loose pictures are photos of J. J. and Mara."

The elderly woman started going through them with shaky hands. "Oh, my . . . this brings back such memories."

"As I told you earlier, Jimmy is obsessed with trying to find his father, and without telling him, Camden and I got in touch with Gary while he was on leave in California. He was unsuccessful, and when you told me that J. J. had changed his name, I realized it wouldn't be possible to find him."

Mrs. King Shu sighed deeply. "Has Jimmy seen these?"

"Not until this morning. He was so sad and discouraged I thought just being able to see what his father looked like might help his morale. I hope I didn't do the wrong thing. He was thrilled to see his father, and asked me if he could have one of the pictures. I told him these belonged to him and he could pick them up at my house after school."

Mrs. King Shu appeared drained by all this. "I have kept as much as I could from Jimmy with good reason. There is nothing worse for a child than to be rejected by his parents. I didn't want that to happen to Jimmy."

"I quite agree. I would never have let it reach that stage. While I was willing to try to find J. J., I would not have told Jimmy unless I knew his father wanted him. You do believe that, don't you?"

"Yes, Katie. I don't think he will be found, but we must protect Jimmy at all costs."

Katie held out her hands to Mrs. King Shu, who grasped them warmly. "We're in this together."

Her weekend date with Camden was different than usual. He had only said that they might just hang out all day Sunday. So she wore comfortable shoes, a jean skirt and a knit shirt, so she would be ready for anything.

"I didn't know what we would be doing, so I guessed this would be okay."

His eyes traveled down to her well-tanned legs. "I wouldn't want you to change a thing." His gaze held warm approval.

There was nothing extra in the car except for the ever-present bottled water. As she glanced at Camden, sitting next to her, she felt very relaxed. On a day like today, the leisurely pace of the tropics lulled her spirit.

He turned the car towards town. "I thought we might go downtown and have lunch at a deli, then we can decide where to go from there. I know a place that makes sandwiches just like a real New York deli. My guess is that the owner moved here from New York."

"That sounds good to me. Of course, they won't be as good as Nina's, but we shouldn't expect that."

He chuckled. "She's something, isn't she?" He turned off the main road and parked next to the deli.

They sat on stools at the counter. As Camden explained, it was so popular on weekdays that there wasn't even a stool available during the lunch hour. The menu was printed on the wall behind the counter, and they turned in their orders.

The sandwiches came with a big dill pickle, chips and coleslaw. Katie took a bite and nodded enthusiastically. "You've done it again, Camden. This is out of this world."

He grinned. "Somehow I knew you'd like it. You know, some women won't eat in a place like this. They have to have fancy salads and things like that."

"Surely all the fellows at the base don't have cars. How do they manage?"

"Most of them don't. They can only go where the bus will take them. I'm lucky because Gary left me his car when he went on to Japan. It makes a big difference."

She finished her sandwich. "Where shall we go from here?"

"Do you like garage sales? There are always lots of them on Sundays. Actually they're mostly junk, but occasionally you find a rare treasure."

"Why not? We're just exploring."

"There's also a little native art shop down here somewhere if I can find it."

"Oh, I'd love that."

They returned to Camden's car, and set off in search of the art shop. "It may not be open on Sunday, but we can check it out anyway."

Finally Camden slowed in a rather shabby neighborhood. "I'm pretty sure this is it," he said, pulling up in front. "My parents had her do a portrait of them from a photograph taken when they were first married. We always loved it, just seeing how they looked when they were young. It has all the earmarks of a Hawaiian picture, rather than a formal portrait."

They stepped out of the car to look at some large paintings that were propped up against the window. One was a portrait of a pretty Hawaiian woman with a lei around her neck, and others that were similar. As they walked through the front yard to get a better view, the front door opened, and the woman from the portrait stuck her head out. "Would you like to come in and see some more pictures?"

"Thanks," Camden said. "We're not serious buyers, we were just admiring the pictures in the window. Did you paint these?"

"Yes." She held the door for them.

Inside, there were about a dozen pictures propped against the walls, and one in production on an easel, turned to the side to catch the north light.

"They're lovely," Katie said, and she meant it. The prices seemed quite reasonable, as well. If only she could afford to buy one. "I can't buy anything right now, but perhaps I'll be able to afford something later."

She turned to Camden. "You know, if you could commission one for Gary, that would be a lovely wedding present."

The artist motioned toward the painting on the easel. "This one was commissioned by a wealthy California man. I'm doing it from a photograph. I usually also like to have one or two sittings, if possible."

They stepped over to get a better look, and their reaction was simultaneous. There was a long moment of stunned silence as they stared at the picture. The only sounds were a dog's playful bark in the backyard, and the rising wind as it blew through a tall palm outside the window.

Chapter Thirteen

The wind continued to blow, as a mid-afternoon storm invaded their tropical paradise. Bits of trash swirled on the road ahead of them as they drove toward Katie's house. There wasn't much chance they would beat the downpour headed their way.

She clutched the artist's card in her hand. The last thing they had expected to see when they stopped by the little art shop was a portrait of J. J. and Mara. There wasn't the slightest doubt in either of their minds that the subject of the portrait was the couple they had become so familiar with through their friendship with Jimmy King Shu.

Katie turned to Camden, concentrating intently on the road ahead through the heavy rain. "When I saw that picture, it was just like encountering a ghost from my past."

"Yes, I felt the same way. It was almost spooky."

There were so many questions. The artist picked up on their interest immediately. "I take it you know this man."

"Yes," Camden replied. "He and my brother were best friends until he moved back to California. Is this a recent commission?"

"I've been working on it for a few weeks, but I think I have a pretty good likeness established. At least, I take it you both recognized him."

Katie couldn't believe their good fortune. "We lost track of him when he moved. Do you happen to have his address handy?"

The artist went to her desk and brought out a ledger. "Here it is. I'll write it down for you."

Camden watched while she wrote, then

took the card. "Thanks. My brother is getting married in California, and I'm sure he will want to invite his friend to the wedding."

The rain started as they made a dash for the car. They looked at each other in stunned disbelief. Camden handed her the card while he started the car. "I take it this is his new name. James King, formerly Jim Jarmond." He drove on back toward Katie's house.

Katie scanned the card. "San Jose. That's in the heart of Silicon Valley."

"Yes, this gets more and more interesting. I can't wait to tell Gary."

Katie nodded. "I'll be interested in hearing what he thinks of all this. You know, Camden, if he is having this portrait done, that tells me he hasn't remarried and that he still loves Mara."

"It looks that way, but that doesn't really add up, either. Surely he wouldn't have rejected her just because he had a chance to make a lot of money."

"Well," Katie said, "to be perfectly realistic, if he didn't want a wife, I hardly think he will want a ten-year-old son."

Camden agreed. "You're probably right,

but that has to be his decision. He has a right to know about his son."

"I guess the important question now is how to approach him. When will Gary be coming through here?"

"I think right away. I'll call him when we get back. Since J. J. knows Gary, I think it would be best to go through him."

"I'm sure he would trust Gary." Katie was thoughtful for a moment. The sound of the windshield wipers going back and forth at full speed momentarily cut into their thoughts.

"Jimmy is so cute, we need to have a picture of him. It would be perfect if we could get one of him with Gary."

"Wouldn't that make Jimmy suspicious? He's awfully smart, you know."

"We'll have to be careful. We can't let him know we've contacted his father."

Camden concentrated on fighting his way through the typhoon-like downpour. It would be such a relief to be back in her driveway, Katie thought. They had to get on with the business of contacting Gary. They were both excited about the possibility of reuniting Jimmy and his father.

Katie urged Camden to be careful.

"This is no time to be swept off the road. I can't wait to get in touch with Gary. Do you think you could e-mail him from my house?"

"We'll try, but he's probably spending the afternoon with his fiancée." Camden laughed. "That sounds funny. I still can't get over the idea of Gary getting married."

At last they reached Katie's house. Camden turned into the driveway, and they made a dash for Katie's back door.

She tossed Camden a towel, and went to work drying her hair and what she could blot off her clothes. "It doesn't look like it will ever stop, does it?"

Camden shook his head. "It feels good to be back at the house. Let's see how much luck we have e-mailing Gary at my parents' house."

They went into her office and turned on her computer. Camden sat down and put in his parents' address, then he typed the message. "Gary, when are you coming through here? Urgent I hear from you immediately. I've found J. J.'s new name and address. If I don't hear from you, I'll call tonight. Send your answer here. I am at

Katie's." He typed in Katie's e-mail address, then sent the message.

Katie suggested they have a snack while they waited. "What would you like? I could fix you some cocoa, or how about a Coke and some popcorn?"

"Yeah, that sounds good." They made some popcorn and opened a couple of Cokes, then went back to her office to enjoy their snack while they waited.

Camden grinned. "You know, there's an old saying, 'a watched computer never boils', or something like that."

"Yes, I know what you mean. I wonder what time it is in California?"

"Around lunch time. We could luck out."

She looked out the window, hoping to see the rain lightening up. "How long can this go on?"

"Actually, I guess it could rain for days, but let's hope it doesn't. I'll have to go back to the base before long."

They had been sitting there long enough to finish their popcorn when they heard the words, "You've got mail." They rushed to the computer.

Gary's message was brief. "Leaving tomorrow. Great news about J. J. See you soon."

Katie and Camden hugged each other in a joyous little victory dance. "We're in luck," Katie crowed. "Can you bring him over here? I'll arrange for him to meet Jimmy after school and we can take some pictures."

"Okay, we'll continue with our plan. You had better alert Mrs. King Shu about what we're doing. I hope she won't object."

"Me too."

"I'd better get back to the base. I'll call you."

Katie followed him to the door. "It looks like it's a little bit lighter, doesn't it?"

"Yeah, it may stop before long." He took her in his arms and his goodbye kiss was unhurried. It told her more than words as he held her close and kissed her over and over again. There was a choked quality to his voice when he told her how hard it was to let her go. "I could hold you like this forever."

How could he ever guess the depth of

her feelings for him? It was far more than she could ever express in mere words.

Nothing was said to Jimmy the following morning when he stopped by to do his chores. "I'm going to take the picture of my dad to school to show my friends," he said.

Katie wondered what kind of questions they would ask. Where was his father? Why didn't he live with him? What was he like? She hoped Jimmy could cope with all those possibilities.

Once he had left, she waited for Nina to arrive before going over to the grocery store. She dreaded telling the news to Mrs. King Shu. It was bound to upset her, but Katie knew it had to be done. If the woman objected, she would just have to talk her into it. Jimmy had a right to have a father, if his father wanted him.

Nina showed up right on time. "I guess Jimmy got his work done today, didn't he? I can tell the porch has been swept off."

"Yes. He was in a good mood, looking forward to showing off a picture of his father. I hope his friends won't ask too many difficult questions."

"How long are you going to keep that kid working to pay off that broken window? It seems to me he's been at it a pretty long time, if it's any of my business."

"It isn't," Katie said with a humorous lift of her eyebrow, "but I happen to like having him around, and I think he likes having an excuse to come by and see me."

"I thought that was it."

"I need to run by the grocery store and have a talk with his grandmother. Can you handle things until I get back?"

"Sure. Take your time."

Mrs. King Shu seemed surprised to see Katie so early in the morning. "Good morning, Katie. Is everything all right?"

"Oh, yes, very much so. I have some news for you. Can you spare a few minutes?"

"Of course. I'll see if my husband can take over here for me." She took a few steps toward the back, and Katie heard her call to him.

In a few moments he made his appearance. "Good morning, Katie. It's good to see you."

Katie gave him a big smile. "How are you this morning?"

"Just fine. My wife is trying to convince me I don't feel well, but she hasn't succeeded yet."

Katie chuckled. "You look fine to me." She followed the little woman to their living quarters.

There was a brief moment when Mrs. King Shu seemed concerned, but she quickly overcame her fear. "I suppose you have some kind of news about Jimmy's father."

"Yes. I happened across it in the most unexpected way." She told Mrs. King Shu about the portrait that he had commissioned in the little art shop. "I got his new name and address. My plan is to have Camden's brother, Gary, write him a letter and enclose a picture of Jimmy taken with Gary. Of course, we will be very careful not to let Jimmy know we have found his father."

Mrs. King Shu could no longer hide her fear. It was creased onto her face, blazing from her eyes. She seemed to shrink physically as she took in the importance of Katie's words. "I guess the worst fear is the fear of the unknown. How will he react? If he wanted his son, how could we let him go?"

Katie put her hand over the little woman's. "I know. Jimmy has to have this chance, though. Don't you see?"

"Yes, I suppose so. Do be careful, Katie."

Chapter Fourteen

After the heavy rain, the humidity was oppressive. When the sun hit the street, it shimmered up in waves of damp heat. *Too bad for the tourists who only have a few days,* Katie thought as she walked back from the grocery store.

She had gone over to reassure Mrs. King Shu and remind her that Jimmy would stop by for a short time after school. The poor woman looked like she had spent a sleepless night, which was no doubt the case. This was a crucial time for all of them.

Nina knew all about what was going

on. "I hope you aren't making a mistake," she said.

"Don't you think I've worried about that often enough? I'm just doing what I believe is the right thing. I can't imagine how it will all turn out, though."

"When are you going to tell the kid?"

"Never, unless I hear that his father is coming for him. As far as Jimmy is concerned, it will be best if he thinks his father's whereabouts are unknown."

It was obvious that Nina didn't approve of her interference, and it could turn out that Nina was right.

It was almost three o'clock when Camden and Gary drove up. She congratulated Gary on his upcoming wedding. "I think you really surprised your brother."

"Yes. I kind of surprised myself. But there comes a time for everyone when they just know the time is right, and that's what happened to me. I'm anxious for you to meet Eve. You are coming to the wedding, aren't you?"

"Camden says I must."

"Good. When does Jimmy get out of school?"

"Three o'clock. I guess Camden briefed

you. He mustn't know we have found his father."

"Don't worry. I'll be careful."

"Let's have some iced tea while we wait for Jimmy," Katie suggested. She got out a pitcher and filled some glasses with ice. "It's a real steam bath out there today, isn't it?"

"Yes, it can get that way sometimes. But it's still better than anywhere else I know of ninety percent of the time."

They sat and visited until Jimmy arrived. Camden introduced Gary while Katie got a glass of lemonade for Jimmy.

"You're the one who knew my dad, aren't you?" Jimmy said.

"Yes, he was a swell guy. We had lots of good times together when we were stationed here."

Jimmy gulped down half his glass of lemonade. "What do you think happened to him?"

Gary shook his head sadly. "I wish I knew."

"I took his picture to school today and showed it to my friends. They all said he was a great-looking guy. Mike wanted to know why I didn't live with him. I just ignored him."

"Good for you," Katie said. She wanted to hug him, but instead suggested they go out and take some pictures. "Camden wants some pictures of Gary before he goes back to Japan."

She took great care placing Gary where the light would be just right. "Okay, now smile." She snapped a couple of pictures.

"How about one of all three of you?" She took a few more snapshots, then one of Camden and Gary, and Gary and Jimmy.

"Jimmy, how about one for me? Give me a big smile. Oh, I like that."

"I just have one more," she said, and with that Camden took the camera. "How about one of the three of you?" He snapped it at the count of three. "That was great."

After that, Katie suggested they go inside for more lemonade. Jimmy had more questions for Gary. "Was there anything unusual about my dad's assignment when he went back to California that last time?"

"No, not at all. We were always being

deployed to different stations, sometimes for just a few days. I didn't think anything of it at the time. It didn't seem unusual until he had been gone for almost a year and I still hadn't heard from him."

"It seems strange that he wouldn't get in touch with my mother, doesn't it?"

"Very strange. He did send her some money, according to your grandmother, but there was only a box number instead of a forwarding address. That was the last they ever heard of him."

"Was that before I was born?"

"Oh, yes. I'm pretty sure he doesn't even know you exist."

"Wow! That's hard to believe."

Katie took the glasses into the kitchen. "Jimmy, I think you had better scoot on home. I wouldn't want your grandmother to worry."

He went back and shook hands with Gary. "I'm glad to have met you." He also shook hands with Camden. "Goodbye."

Katie walked to the door with him. "I'll show you the pictures when we get them developed. See you later."

Gary grinned at Katie. "His grandparents certainly taught him some manners, didn't they?"

"Yes, you can see why I've become so attached to him. If his father ever met him I'm sure he wouldn't be able to resist him."

"Well," Camden said, "we're doing the best we can. The rest is up to fate."

Katie smiled. "I'd say fate has done her part steering us to that little art shop. I have a suggestion, Gary. When you send your letter to J. J. with the pictures, why don't you give him my e-mail address? That might speed things up a bit."

"Good idea. I'll be gone by the time he gets that letter."

Camden and Gary had to return to the base. "I'll drop the pictures off to be developed on the way," Camden said. "They should be ready by tonight. Can you go out to eat with us tonight?"

"Sure. What time?"

They made the plans and she saw them off. Her spirits soared just thinking about what they might accomplish in the next few days.

The rest of the day, Katie forced herself to keep her mind on her business. It wasn't easy, since she kept imagining a reunion between Jimmy and his father. She reminded herself over and over not to think of it. *You're in for a big disappointment if you aren't careful.*

About a quarter to seven Camden and Gary appeared, swearing they were close to starvation, not having eaten anything for several hours.

Katie laughed and offered them a plate of hors d'oeuvres, consisting of some Asiago cheese toasts and a dish of pico de gallo.

Gary turned to Camden with a glint of humor in his eyes. "This woman is obviously a gourmet cook. Don't let her get away."

Camden laughed. "That's good advice, although it does seem odd coming from such a loner. I was beginning to think you'd be a bachelor for the rest of your life."

Katie stepped into the breach. "Where are we going to eat tonight?"

"Maybe we should let Gary decide, since he's the guest."

"I'd love to have some steak," Gary

said. "Is there a good steak house near here?"

"Sure. How does that suit you, Katie?"

She nodded. "I already had myself prepared for it, knowing that's what both of you guys would want."

Before long, they were seated at a casual steak house, enjoying their meal.

Camden reached into his pocket. "Before I forget, we stopped on the way and picked up the pictures." He handed the envelope to Katie.

She looked through them, stopping to gaze at one or two. "Look at this." She held out a picture of Jimmy and Gary. "If Jimmy's father can resist this one, he isn't human."

"Yes," Gary agreed, "he's one cute kid." He fished into his pocket and handed Katie the letter he had written to go with it. "What do you think of this?"

Katie read it carefully, then handed it back to him. "I like it. It's brief, to the point, and non-judgmental."

"Good. I'll drop it in a mailbox when we leave here."

After that, they concentrated on their food, which was well-prepared and satisfying. As they were leaving, Katie remarked that she was glad they had been spared from imminent starvation once again.

They found a mailbox and dropped J. J.'s letter in. Once they reached her house, they said goodbye. "I'll be returning to Japan tomorrow," Gary told her, "so I guess I'll see you next at the wedding."

Katie waved them off cheerily, after Camden gave her a quick goodbye kiss.

Three days passed before they had a response from Gary's letter. It had been three days during which the thought of Jimmy's father seldom left Katie's mind.

She had gone into her office to check her e-mail before going to bed. She turned on her computer, waited to get online, and typed in her password.

Her heart started pounding unbearably as soon as she heard the words: "You've got mail." With trembling hands, she opened her in-box.

Can't wait to see my son. Arriving in my own plane mid-afternoon tomorrow. James

Chapter Fifteen

Even though it was late, Katie called Mrs. King Shu and said she had news for her. She insisted on delivering it in person, and walked over to the grocery store.

The store was closed, but the couple waited to let her in. Mrs. King Shu looked pale. "It's Jimmy's father, isn't it?"

"Yes. He will arrive tomorrow to see his son."

The little woman swayed slightly, and her husband put his arm around her. "Perhaps we should go back where we can sit down."

Katie changed into soft slippers and

followed the King Shus to their living quarters.

"I know this is a terrible shock. It was for me, too. I think you should be the ones to tell Jimmy. You can write a note to his teacher asking that he be let out early. Camden and I will pick him up at school so he can meet the plane. Will you go with us?"

Mrs. King Shu looked bewildered. "This is so sudden. I don't know what to say." She looked at her husband, who appeared equally bewildered. "Perhaps we had better stay here. I'm not sure we want to see him."

Katie nodded, understanding. "You can call me if you change your mind."

The following morning Jimmy showed up at Katie's house. He was so excited, he was practically walking two feet off the ground. "Can you believe it? My dad is flying in this afternoon! It all happened so suddenly. You found him for me, didn't you?"

"I wouldn't have if you hadn't been so anxious to find him. You deserve all the credit for that, and I just hope you won't be disappointed. We don't really know what to expect, do we?"

"Don't worry, Katie. He'll be a swell guy. I just know it."

There was nothing she could say to dispel his excitement. He would just have to face whatever the future brought. "Do you have your note for the teacher?"

"Yes." He patted the back of his jeans. "Right here."

"Good. Camden and I will pick you up at two-thirty. I asked your grandparents to go with us, but they decided to stay home."

"Yeah, they didn't feel too well this morning."

Jimmy looked up at the attic. "All this happened because I climbed up and brought down that box, didn't it?"

"Yes. You see Jimmy, *you're* the one who found him."

Jimmy started to take the trash out. Katie chuckled. "I think you've done enough work to pay for two or three broken windows. Anytime you want to skip your chores, it's all right with me."

"Oh, I don't mind."

* * *

By two-thirty Katie was caught up on her work. Nina promised to stay until closing time in case any orders came in. "I hope everything works out all right," she said. "I can see you're nervous."

"Yes, I must admit I am worried. I'm also excited and determined to be optimistic."

Camden was right on time. As they were leaving, he called out, "Wish us luck, Nina."

"I hope everything turns out the way you want it to."

Once they were on the way to the school, Camden turned to Katie. "You're nervous, aren't you?"

"Yes, more than I've ever been. I hope I've done the right thing."

"We'll soon find out. He didn't waste any time once he got the letter, did he?"

"No, and that's encouraging."

The wait at the airport was suspenseful. With every plane that landed, Jimmy jumped up and went to the window. "Is that my dad?"

They must have waited at least half an hour when the largest private plane they had ever seen landed. "I think that's it," Jimmy said. As it taxied into position, they watched. The next thing they saw took them all by surprise.

Two men stepped out onto the ramp, then went back inside. They returned with a wheelchair, and carefully wheeled it onto the ramp. The man sitting in the wheelchair could not be seen clearly until he made his way into the waiting room.

Katie watched Jimmy's expression carefully. His eyes were big and round as he digested the implications of what he saw. "That's my dad," he said quietly.

Camden stepped forward to greet him. "I'm Gary's brother, Camden."

"James King. This is Terryl Chronister, my pilot, and Wayne Harman, my nurse." They shook hands.

Camden led them over to where Katie and Jimmy waited. "This is my friend, Katie Weston, and this is your son, Jimmy."

Katie watched as Jimmy continued to stare. She spoke first. "Welcome to Honolulu," she said, then nudged Jimmy. He stepped forward and thrust his hand out to shake hands. "Hello, Dad."

She saw James' throat work as he swallowed hard. "I'm sure you weren't expecting to find me disabled. We'll have to get acquainted now. I have lots to tell you."

He turned to Camden. "Thanks for meeting my plane. We'll rent a van and Terryl will drive us in. I'll be staying at the Halekalaini. Shall we meet at your house?"

"Yes. Come on over as soon as it's convenient. We'll be expecting you."

"I'd also like to meet with the King Shus. Could you arrange that?"

"I'll call them as soon as we get back."

Jimmy was quiet as they drove back to Katie's house. Finally Katie spoke. "I know you weren't expecting to find your father in a wheelchair. We'll have to find out just what happened to him, shall we?"

"Okay," Jimmy said in a small voice.

Apparently it would be up to Jimmy's father to win him over. Camden spoke up. "Be patient, Jimmy. We all need a little time to get acquainted."

Once they reached Katie's house, she phoned the King Shus and explained that Jimmy's father wanted to meet with them. She also told them they should be prepared for the fact that he was a paraplegic.

Katie prepared some tea for the King Shus as soon as they arrived.

They were all braced for what they would hear from James King. When they arrived, his driver and nurse insisted on waiting in the van.

James went immediately to the King Shus and reached out for their hands. "I want you to know that my fondness for you never wavered. I know you must have thought harshly of me, and I don't blame you."

He turned to the others in the room. "Before anything else, I owe you all an explanation. I was deployed to San Diego on a routine assignment. Coming in from the airport I was in a terrible accident, a collision between my taxi and a large van with two passengers."

He shook his head to dispell the image that ran through his mind of the moment just before the accident. "As far as the accident itself is concerned, I don't have any memory at all. I was the only survivor, and I was unconscious for quite some time."

James paused as he took a sip of the lemonade Katie had provided. "When I came to, it was several days before I realized I had no feeling from the waist down. My doctor explained that my condition was caused by a spinal cord injury, and that I would be paralyzed."

His eyes focused on the frosted glass as he tried to hold his emotions under control. "I wanted Mara by my side . . . oh, how I missed her."

Now his gaze turned to the King Shus. "Mara was the kind of wife who would devote her life to me, would wait on me, and ask nothing in return for herself. But that was not the kind of life I wanted for her. She deserved so much more. She was a warm, vibrant person. I reasoned that if she knew nothing about what happened to me, she would eventually make a life of her own. That is why I disappeared."

There was absolute silence in the room. Mrs. King Shu dabbed at her eyes, and waited quietly for him to resume his story.

"I was awarded a large settlement for my injury. I sent as much money to Mara as I could at the time, using a post office box as a return address."

"The next thing I did was to contact my cousin, who had gone to high school with me. We had both been interested in engineering, so after high school he went on to Stanford, but since I wanted to follow my family tradition in the Navy, I went to Annapolis. Except for Christmas cards, we've had very little contact since then.

"My decision to contact him turned out to be the right move on my part. After all those years, he was the only person I could turn to, and he didn't let me down. He had made a brilliant career for himself in technology, and he urged me to come to San Jose. In fact, he took me under his wing, I invested some of my settlement in his company, and before I knew it, we were sharing ideas just like we had in high school. Larry is a good friend.

"I could see I would soon be a very wealthy man, so I sent more money to Mara. She had never been out of my thoughts. When my letter was returned with the word "Deceased" stamped on it, I went into a real depression. Even though I had made my fortune, I lost hope that I would ever find true happiness in my life."

He turned and smiled at Jimmy. "As soon as I got Gary's letter with Jimmy's picture in it, my spirits soared. You can't imagine the joy I felt. That was the first time I found out that Mara had become pregnant before I left . . ."

Mrs. King Shu interrupted. "She didn't know until you left that she was pregnant."

James paused and took a swig of his lemonade. "Of course, I can't expect my son to accept a perfect stranger the minute he meets him, so I know we'll need time to become acquainted. I'm prepared to stay here several weeks and work out all the details with my in-laws."

He turned to the King Shus. "You've done a good job of raising Jimmy so far, and I would never dream of taking him away from you after all this time. I have a very nice guest house I'd like to offer you. It has two bedrooms, a living room, and a kitchenette. We could sell the grocery store, and I would see to it that you are well taken care of."

Mrs. King Shu turned to her husband and reached out her hand to him. "What do you think, dear?"

James spoke up. "I don't want you to make a decision right away. Talk it over, and let me know when you've made up your minds. In fact, if you would like to bring Jimmy over in my plane for a little visit, you could see for yourself what it would be like."

Jimmy was beginning to warm up. "Could I have a basketball goal?"

"Oh, I already have one, and if I do say so myself, I'm a pretty good player. I can make a basket from just about any angle."

Jimmy grinned. "So can I."

This delighted James. "Wayne plays a round with me every morning before work, but he's a lousy player."

"My friend says I'm too short to play basketball, but he's not too good himself."

James snorted. "That's a lot of nonsense. I'm shorter than you in my wheelchair, but I can play rings around Wayne. I think we could have some pretty good games, don't you?"

Jimmy grinned. "You bet."

After everyone had left, Camden helped Katie load everything into the dishwasher. "It went pretty well, didn't it?"

"Yes. I don't think there's much doubt

that all three of them will go to San Jose to look things over. I'd be very surprised if three more residents didn't move into Silicon Valley before very long."

Camden showed up for his usual lunch with Katie on Saturday. "Where's Nina?"

"She went to deliver a cake for a big wedding tonight. I told her I could deliver it, but she insisted, saying I shouldn't rush you off after lunch."

Camden smiled. "That was considerate of her." He helped himself to a second sandwich. "Of course, I always enjoy having her eat with us, but it's even better when I have you all to myself."

Katie noticed he seemed to be in an exceptionally good mood. "I guess you're feeling good about our success in finding Jimmy's father. I know I am."

"Me too. Mrs. King Shu called this morning. She sounded like a changed person. They're very excited about the prospect of going to San Jose to look over the setup there. She said Jimmy just couldn't wait."

They finished lunch, and Camden carried the dishes in and loaded the dishwasher. Since he usually rushed off about this time, Katie was puzzled. "Don't you have to return to the base this afternoon?"

"Not today. I took the rest of the day off for some important business."

"Oh, really? If you don't mind telling me, what's so important?"

"It's personal."

"Oh, pardon me for asking."

"That's all right. I'll need your assistance."

She gave him a curious look. "I'm at your service. Would you like some cookies for dessert?"

"No, thanks." He finished loading the dishwasher and wiping off the counters.

"Okay, now you have my complete attention. What's on your mind?"

He turned her toward him and drew her close, and kissed her. His arms encircled her, holding her so tightly she couldn't move. "Oh, how I love you," he breathed when he finally came up for air.

Then, before she could speak, she felt his hands on her face, his tender kiss once more taking possession of her. Katie relaxed in the exquisite pleasure of his embrace.

Camden was still holding her close when the door opened and Nina's voice squeaked. "Oh, excuse me." She quickly closed the door.

"We probably embarrassed her," Katie said, smiling guiltily. Reluctantly, she pushed herself away from him.

"I don't think so. Nina is such a romantic, she will be thrilled to death." Camden said with a big grin. "I love you," he said in a loud voice. "It's no secret."

Katie giggled. "I love you, too." She lifted her face for another kiss. He brushed her forehead with soft little kisses; then she saw his face was wreathed in a smile. "What are you smiling about?"

"I just happened to think how happy my mother would be if both her bachelor boys got married."

"Both? You mean . . ."

"Katie, will you marry me?"

"Well, just a minute now . . . how do I know you're not just trying to keep up with your brother? You two *are* awfully competitive."

"I swear, Gary has nothing to do with it. I already knew I wanted to marry you before I ever heard that Gary was getting married. Will you, Katie?"

"Mmmm . . . and how do I know that Alicia Bronfman won't surface again?"

"Forget her. She's gone back to California. I finally convinced her she was out of the picture."

"And what if your parents can't stand me? What then?"

"That's impossible. I promise they'll love you. So will you, Katie? Will you marry me?"

She smiled, her heart overflowing. "*Yes* I'll marry you. I thought you'd never ask."

He heaved a sigh of relief, and his kiss said more than words ever could. He reached into his pocket and pulled out a box. "Hold out your finger."

The diamond ring he slipped onto her finger blazed with the reflected fire in her heart, a fire that would burn brightly forever.